It Should Have Been You

A Rekindled Romance Novel

CHERYL BARTON

Dedication

To those who believe in unconditional, everlasting, happily ever after endings. This one's for you!

To the memory of Teddy Pendergrass who wrote one of the most perfect love songs, *"It Should Have Been You"*. It's one of my favorites.

<u>**Stand Alone Romance**</u>
Snowbound
Cupid's Arrow
One Wish
His Halloween Promise
Holly for Christmas
A Better Man
Bossy
Un-Break My Heart
Love on Top
Take a Knee
Love at First Sight
My First Love
Black Love
*A Younger
Man*
The Lake House
True Lies or True Love
When I Think of You
Baby, Come Back
Unforgettable
The Power of Seduction
Seize the Moment
A Christmas Wish

"Sometimes you have to let life turn you upside down, so you can learn how to live right side up."
– Not Easily Broken (2009)

1

The hospital. *This freaking hospital!*

Standing in the middle of his favorite on-call room, Dr. Clayton Myers was caught with someone he shouldn't be with in a place that was as much a home for him as his actual home. In the midst of what was about to be yet another indiscretion, the one saving grace is that they were fully clothed when they were caught by the last person he ever wanted to hurt. Today, not only was the woman he'd been sneaking around with, Michelle, a nurse, smiling as if she was happy they were interrupted, but when the door slowly creaked opened and then closed, shocking him into reality, in front of him stood the love of his life and fellow doctor, Donna Johnson.

This was the last place Clayton expected his lies and deceit to come full circle, but here he was, angrier at himself than he's ever been. He thought he was being discreet about his deeds, but Donna's presence disputed that notion.

The consequence of his choices shoved him into reality; a place he wished he could go back to in his recent past and change. Facing the error of his ways in a space where he came to fix lives while his own life was about to crumble was not how he planned for his day to go. He needed to sweat off some stress before a major surgery, but it was clear, he once again chose the wrong person to do it with. Being a major screw-up made this encounter inevitable. He couldn't explain away what Donna's eyes were taking in. He was caught red-handed with the bottom half of his scrubs already untied while his hands were well on their way to yanking them down his legs. What he and Michelle were about to do was obvious.

The hospital is where the idea was to pump life back into a body that wasn't doing its best. Here he was trying to figure out how to do the same for a relationship he was sure was collapsing because he'd been stupid. The hurt on Donna's face told him that there would be no lifesaving efforts in his future; he was done. The corpse that was his relationship was about to be dead and buried and it was his own fault.

No words were spoken as she looked from him to Michelle and then back to him. He was screwed, and not in the good way. He inwardly kicked himself for that last thought. It was how he found himself in this mess in the first place. He had months to come clean and to even stop his behavior, but now it was too late. Not only had Donna walked in on them, but he was certain that his greatest deed was about to come to the surface. His carelessness had come full circle and his life was coming apart in the very place where he'd snuck away to on several occasions with women that were not Donna. The fact that Michelle wasn't the first woman he cheated with wasn't a good example of who a fiancé should be.

Silence. That was the worse about this moment. Donna's eyes were like laser beams, piercing through him, no doubt in her mind, stabbing him in the heart. The scene before her had done just that to her.

The white hospital walls fell away, the smell of strong hospital cleaning solutions seemed putrid to his nostrils and the room seemed to get smaller and smaller with every minute they stood across from each other. He wanted to tear down and burn the beds he could see out of the corner of his eye. He'd caught Donna checking them out as his lies and his truths faced them all. How did she find him? Today was her day off. He was hoping to have some time to talk to Michelle and then to Donna before news got around the hospital. Soon, his secret would no longer be a secret. He didn't want it to come out this way.

Clayton should be riding high now that he has finally completed his surgical residency at Johns Hopkins Hospital in Baltimore, Maryland. He should be on cloud nine and preparing for a night of celebrating with Donna. Months earlier, they were celebrating their engagement after he planned out the perfect proposal with their family and friends in attendance. Though they hadn't met until medical school, he and Donna were both from Texas, where their families had traveled from. He was sure the engagement was all but done. If he were going to have any chance of saving the little bit of his relationship with Donna that he thought he could resuscitate, he was going to have to come clean about everything; not just about Michelle.

She told him a few weeks ago that she was pregnant and that the baby was his. To say that he was disgusted with himself would be an understatement.

Timing was everything and Donna's was perfect; or not, Clayton thought. He was in the middle of listening to Michelle give him an ultimatum that either he tells Donna or she would just before she offered him one last romp if he wanted it. She wanted to show him what he would be missing if he chose Donna over her. He was just stupid enough to let his ego lead him to accept her offer when the door opened. This was not how he saw this going down.

The silence was killing him. He didn't know whether to explain to Donna what she was seeing or to ask Michelle to leave so that he could talk to Donna in private.

"Well, look who just happens to show up!" Michelle exclaimed, breaking the uncomfortable silence.

Clayton tried with all of his might to find words to explain what was happening.

"Donna, listen, honey – I can explain what you're seeing," he tried to explain.

When her eyes went from him and landed on Michelle again, Clayton didn't know what was coming next; he waited.

"Happen to show up? That's how you explain sending a message for me to come to this very on-call room at this very moment?" Donna asked her.

"What?" Clayton yelled. "I did no such thing. I thought you were off today," he told her, reaching for her as she took a step away from him.

Clayton turned to Michelle when she raised her hand as if she were in high school asking permission to speak.

"I may have done that. Trust me, it was for your own good. You needed to know what was going on and Clayton was taking too long to tell you. Time is of the essence!" Michelle asserted while gloating.

He'd been had. Michelle had set this up.

"Time is of what essence? For what you were about to do? Am I early for the show or are you working on getting dressed?" Donna asked, eyeing them.

"Not at all. You're just in time for what's already happened and the result is this," Michelle slyly slurred out as she rubbed her hand across her flat stomach, making it clear that the three of them being here together wasn't some kind of coincidence.

When Clayton turned his head in her direction again, he was appalled at her display of heartlessness.

To hone in on her point, Michelle raised her top, showing the underside of her bra-covered breasts. That's not where she was pointing with the hand that wasn't holding up her shirt. Michelle's index finger was pointing at her yet expanding belly, but it wouldn't look that way much longer.

When Donna inhaled loudly, eyes bulging with her eyes planted on Michelle's midriff, Clayton didn't know how to run things back to where he could talk to Donna about this in private, in a more caring manner than the selfish way in which Michelle had just blurted out the secret he'd been holding back.

"Clayton? What is she talking about and what is it that you need to explain?" Donna asked.

"This! Look, I know this isn't the best way to tell you, but Clayton should have come clean to you by now or our child will be here in seven months. You may not want to find out that he's a father by the appearance of a child. Tell her Clayton. We've been sneaking around long enough," Michelle continued.

Clayton stood like a statue hoping the moment would turn out to be a dream. He wanted to look back at Donna. He really wanted to, but there were no words that would explain away the revelation that just came out of Michelle's mouth.

"Michelle, get out! You didn't have to do that," he shouted.

"No, Michelle, don't leave. If what you're saying is true, my *fiancé* should have told you to get out way before this moment. Is that what you've been doing? I mean, I've heard rumors for a long time and I've ignored them all," Donna acknowledge.

"Oh, so you know your fiancé is a man-whore? I mean, who doesn't know? This nurse, that nurse; this doctor, that doctor. His reckless decisions with a sexy pharmaceutic representative here and there. Too many to count, right Clayton? Tell her! Tell her about the many times we've slipped away to this very room. You've been here with him too, right? I think I've heard the moans a time or two."

Michelle laughed out loud, practically reacting to what she saw as her knee-slapping humor. Clayton was furious, but he had to keep his cool and focus on Donna, not Michelle.

Knowing how Michelle could be at tongue-lashing, he turned to Donna and blocked her view of Michelle.

"Listen, baby, I'm so sorry for everything. Let me explain," Clayton said, now focused and fighting for his life and their love. They could make it through this; they had to. He was heading to Baylor University Medical Center in Dallas, Texas, as a new surgical attending. Donna still had a year of residency left and he needed to reassure her that with him in Texas and her in Maryland, they could still have their future together despite him being messy.

"You got her pregnant?" Donna screamed.

"I can explain."

"You can explain *what*? Sleeping with her and

countless others?"

"Oh, we weren't sleeping at all," Michelle chimed in.

"You shut up, you..." Donna yelled at Michelle.

"Donna don't. Listen, ignore her right now and focus on me," Clayton interjected.

Through his surgical scrub top, he could feel the sweat forming like pools of water under his arms. This was as bad as things could get for him. The anger and hurt in the eyes of the woman he'd loved for the past three years was evident. If she decided to pick up something and hit him with it, he was ready and deserving of it. He'd made the biggest mistake of his life. What he had with Donna was ruined if he couldn't make his apology mean enough for her to forgive him.

"I'm sorry; it just happened," he offered, in a soft tone to calm the moment.

"What just happened? You sort of bumped uglies with nurse-in-training Michelle and she somehow, miraculously got pregnant! How could you? I thought we had something. I guess the rumors are true that you've been messing around with nurses at the hospital; right here where we both work and she's pregnant?"

Trying to calm the situation he reached for Donna knowing he only had one chance to make things right and prove that they can still have a relationship, even a marriage, if she would just forgive his slip up.

"I've been foolish and I got caught up," he

admitted.

"No, what you did is the same thing the rest of the males around here are doing, which is sneaking off to the on-call rooms with every nurse who wiggles her behind your way. This isn't some episode of a popular television medical drama. You get that, right? This is my life you're messing with. How could you do this to me and with her? Are you sure it's yours? She has just as much of a reputation as you do. You both make me sick!" Donna screamed.

"No need to send your anger my way. It was up to you to keep your man happy enough to keep him from straying!" Michelle yelled in defense.

Clayton saw it coming and he was happy that he braced himself to intervene.

Before Donna could get close enough to tackle Michelle to the floor, he grabbed her mid-flight as she lunged forward. She was no doubt going for Michelle's neck. He couldn't allow violence because of his stupidity. He watched as Michelle moved back out of Donna's reach and cowered in a corner, her eyes protruding in fear. The usual motor-mouth that Michelle used as her defense was silenced at the fear of death standing in front of her in the form of a five-foot, seven-inch-tall doctor who he knew could flatten Michelle like a pancake. Donna was shorter and thinner, to Michelle's five-foot, nine-inch frame and thicker all around, but Donna was in rare form. She was a woman scorned and embarrassed and Michelle had too much mouth. He had to keep them apart.

"Michelle, just shut the hell up; I got this," he demanded.

"True and I got this!" Michelle replied, once again pointing to her stomach. "I expect you to protect our child from this crazy woman! Get her out of here before she does something that could endanger our child's welfare," Michelle added.

"Leave!" Donna yelled. "Leave now!" she screamed at Michelle.

Clayton had never seen Donna this angry and he knew the best thing right now was to separate them.

At age twenty-nine, he didn't think he'd be having any children yet. He and Donna had decided to wait a few years to have kids after she completed her residency and joined him in Texas. Her plan was to practice pediatric surgery at any one of the large hospitals in Dallas that he knew were already recruiting her. He was looking forward to starting their life in Dallas until she could join him. He saw those dreams fading away with each second. The anger and stiffness he felt in Donna's body as he held her back from Michelle spoke volumes.

"Well, I'm only leaving because it's clear the two of you need to figure this out. Clayton, you know where to find me when you're done. I'll be at my apartment. You know that place that you've been to many times late-night?" Michelle said facetiously.

Clayton once again held onto Donna tight as he felt

her lunge in Michelle's direction again.

"Get out!" Donna yelled again and this time, the walls of the room vibrated; they all felt it. Even Michelle looked around at how the octave in the room made things move without a touch.

Clayton turned to ask Michelle to leave, but he didn't have to. He watched her stumble over a metal chair as she dashed for the other door in the room. When it shut behind her, Clayton opened his arms and let go of Donna who struggled fiercely against his hold. He then stepped back to give her room and remained quiet. He watched her shuffle her feet out of rage and frustration. She reached for her head, placing her palm flat against her forehead with the other hand on her blue scrub-covered hip.

"Baby, let's talk this out calmly and let me explain how stupid I am."

"Don't you dare play victim by claiming stupidity. You knew exactly what you were doing. You have been cheating on me for a long time. I looked the other way because love blinded me. This is what you do to me? To us? There are no excuses here. You are about to have a baby with another woman and I'm standing here with the engagement ring you gave me on my finger. This ring came with a promise to love me and only me!" she avowed.

Clayton kept his eyes on the ring that she now waved back and forth in front of his face, reminding him of the day he'd placed it there. They had been happy that night, but not so much now.

"Donna, I do love you and only you. I messed up. I don't love Michelle."

"Oh, you think that makes it okay? You had casual sex with her, who knows how many times and yet, you can still utter that you love me. I must look stupid to you. I'm the one who's sorry. I'm sorry that I let my love overshadow the trust and faith I didn't have in you, but I put in my pocket to one day throw away once we were married and you were finished sowing your oats. I got it. You're a big time resident and a chick magnet. You're an extremely handsome black man who is also brilliant with a bright future; a man any woman would love to have as her own. I fell victim to all of that. I thought that you would curtail your desire for other women once we were engaged and married, but there is no fixing you. You're a *dog* and you always will be one. I can't believe I continually fell for one lie after the other when I would hear that you were seen coming out of rooms all over this hospital, pulling up your scrubs and then right after, a nurse or other female doctor would exit the same room straightening her clothes as well. I'm so *stupid*!" she yelled.

"You're not. I'm the stupid one. I love you Donna and I'm sorry that my wayward penis has more control over me than my heart," he said and then regretted the words. The blank stare on Donna's face told him that those were not the right words to say.

"What an awful situation you've created. What?

Am I supposed to continue working around her as she gets bigger and everyone knows the baby is yours? Oh, right, you won't have to worry about that because you're heading to Texas. How selfish of you to not think before you slip and slide into one woman after another. You slept with her with no condom? You have to know that you are not the only guy around here that she's been known to slide into a room with. What the hell were you thinking?" she yelled.

Clayton lowered his head in shame.

"I've never slept with a woman without a condom. It broke or something," he solemnly admitted.

"So, you're sure it's yours?" she asked.

"No, I don't, but I think it may be. She claims that since we started messing around, there hasn't been anyone else other than me."

"How many times did you screw her? Ten? Twenty? More than that?" she pleaded.

Clayton exhaled, not wanting to lie while also not ready to be truthful.

"I don't know how many times. It's been going on for about six months," he admitted.

"What? You were doing her before you proposed to me in front of my family and yours? The engagement party was five months ago."

"Baby, I'm sorry," he said, reaching for her.

"Don't you dare touch me. Don't ever touch me again. I hope it was worth it. I hope cheating on me, making me look and feel like a fool and having everyone snicker about me behind my back and in my face, gets you through life. Whatever life we had together, it's done. Good luck in Texas. Never speak to me again!"

"Wait, we can make it through this. I will do anything you want, just don't give up on us yet," he begged.

"Me? You don't want me to give up on us? You did! You gave up on us every time you slipped in here with her and other women or when you made a late-night run to Michelle's apartment. I can't with you right now. I'm going to be sick. I have to get out of here."

Before he could plead his case further in order to retain the life they had been planning together, his words ended in the back of his throat when Donna removed her diamond engagement ring and threw it in his face. After hitting his forehead, the ring fell to the floor, rolled a few times and stopped. He would have reached for it and begged her to keep it on her finger until they could talk with leveler heads, but he never got the chance. He looked in her direction, but she had already slipped out of the door. Defeated, he moved backwards and sat down on the twin bed behind him.

Clayton closed his eyes to take it all in. He had just lost the love of his life. He'd taken her love for granted by getting caught up in his status as a surgical resident, an appealing title to every woman he came across. He got caught up in the interest and the fun of it when all the while, he should have kept his mind and body on

Donna. Now, what was he going to do? He had a feeling she was never going to forgive him. If that was the case, he had nothing and after what he did to their lives, that's exactly what he deserved.

2

Twelve Years Later

Packing and unpacking for a move from New York to Texas was no easy task. Dr. Donna Spencer discovered a new hatred for everything surrounding moving, something she's done more than a few times in her life. Here she was again, after her last and hopefully final move, unpacking the boxes in the master bedroom suite of her newly purchased three-bedroom, four-bath ranch-style home.

Pulling off a massive move for herself and her nine-year-old daughter, Zoe, was finally snatching the wind from her lungs. Boxes and clothes were everywhere as she looked at the mayhem in her room. What bothered her the most was the idea that she'd been in her home for two-months and other than a few boxes unpacked to be sure she and Zoe had clothes to wear, she still had the rest of the house to unpack.

Thankfully, she was back in Texas, in Dallas and not in Fort Worth, where she grew up thirty minutes away. That was where her sister, Candace Parker and parents Randolph and Sallie Johnson, still lived. She was happy to finally be closer to them and not over sixteen hundred miles away like when she lived in Maryland, during her time as a resident at Johns Hopkins hospital. After a fumble in her life called getting married on a dare, she had then moved to New York City where she continued her career as a pediatric surgeon. In all of the years that she spent away from Texas, nothing really felt like home until her feet touched back down in the state that she loved so much.

The best decision she'd ever made in her life was accepting the position as a Pediatric Surgeon at Children's Health Systems of Texas in Dallas, a teaching hospital. She loved the world of medicine and most of all, she loved research when it came to pediatric advancements and teaching new doctors who have a passion for helping the world's littlest patients.

In her most comfortable black yoga pants and her favorite pink and white striped crop top, she looked around her room where her eyes landed on her king-size bed, with its silver tufted headboard. The bed was covered in her new pink and white comforter set that matched the pink, silver and white décor. She smiled at how much she and her daughter were alike, especially when it came to matching bedroom colors. Zoe's room symbolized more of that little girl who loved dolls look while hers was bougie and bling, as her sister Candace called it on her first visit from Fort Worth over a month ago. She visited to help with the unpacking, but they didn't get much done once Candace opened a bottle of wine. Unpacking then became an after-thought.

With Zoe at school enjoying the last two weeks in her new school, she was hoping to get a lot done after uprooting their lives this close to the end of the school year. She had planned to wait until Zoe had finished out the school year in New York but then decided that it would be best to allow her at least a month or so of making new friends that she could remain friends with over the summer. With Zoe being an only child and moving to Dallas, leaving a lifetime of friends behind was already going to be an adjustment. The greatest plus to accepting the job and moving was that Zoe would once again live close to her father, Benny, his new wife, Alicia and his parents who all lived minutes away.

There was already so much change in their lives when she divorced Benny when they lived in New York. Their quickie marriage had been in jeopardy from the moment they said *I do*. They had Zoe, whom they both loved, but loving each other had never been a part of the equation. During their separation before the divorce, Benny took a job as a morning talk show producer in Dallas where he'd grown up. When they first met, they vibed over the fact that they were both from Texas and living in Baltimore. It reminded her of how she and Clayton had connected back then.

In Baltimore, Benny was the producer of an early

morning news segment of the number one news show in that market. That was back when they'd met after her life and crashed and burned during the fourth year of her five-year surgical residency.

Though the divorce was amicable, there were still strained points between them, especially after he left and she decided to stay. She had done enough moving around, leaving Maryland to follow him to New York for his big job opportunity. With the divorce, she needed her own fresh outlook on life and decided to spend another two years in New York before deciding on a move that she'd tossed around for six months. She felt some type of way about the move to Texas knowing that there was the possibility she would run into the one and only man she'd ever truly loved; that man wasn't Benny. That man was Dr. Clayton Myers, who was now a world-known chief of surgery, who had performed some of the riskiest, yet remarkable surgeries. They would be at two different hospitals, but avoiding each other all together would be a stretch.

Turning away from the destruction in her room, she walked out and headed downstairs to try and tackle unpacking more of her home office.

Checking out her office with rose gold walls and white and rose gold furniture, she admired the girlie look of it. Happy that she had at least set up wireless speakers in various rooms, including her office, she clicked away at the keys on her iPad until the sweet sounds of Teddy Pendergrass cascaded throughout the room. His music was a great motivator as she swayed and reached for boxes.

As she opened box after box, she found the one with her degrees, preferring to keep them at home rather than in her office at the hospital. Pulling out one framed certificate after another, it wasn't until she got to the very bottom that she sat on the brown hardwood floor, crossed her legs and held her medical school degree in her hands. That had been the happiest time in her life and she felt as if her life had been running on roller skates ever since. To most, that was the life of a doctor, but to her, she wanted some time to slow down and enjoy more time with Zoe who was growing up too fast. As an attending at a teaching hospital, she was hoping to have more time to balance work and time at home, better hours and more time that she could devote to research. That was the agreement she made with the hospital before she accepted the job. They had given her full reign over her career.

She thought back to when life seemed simpler back in medical school. She barely slept but she dealt with it because outside of work as an intern then resident after medical school, she had also been deeply in love with a man she thought she would spend the rest of her life with. Clayton had been her whole world. What she also discovered was that he was also the only person in the world who could make her feel a pain in her heart that she never thought she would recover from. So much uncertainty had happened as a result of what he took her through, getting another woman pregnant while engaged to her.

After his betrayal, she'd fallen into the arms of Benny as a rebound affair, hoping to feel wanted and loved again. That had been her first big mistake. Her second had been marrying Benny after four months of dating. A couple of years later, the one bright spot of her marriage was the day she found out she was pregnant. Making up for a marriage that hadn't worked well from the first day, she put her love and energy into Zoe and so had Benny. They spent years doing that until they realized the love for their daughter was all they had. One deep discussion from the heart and they confessed that not only were they not in love with each other, they never had been.

Back then, Benny had been coming off of a bad breakup at the same time that she was suffering through Clayton's lies and betrayal. After a few casual dates, something she needed at the time and all that she could handle, they ran off to Las Vegas for a quick wedding. They both regretted the spur of the moment decision but never shared that with each other until years later when they finally separated. Instead of admitting the lack of real love at the moment, they lived as friends and lovers, while not being in love. She cared for Benny and in her own way, she always would, but it wasn't the heart pounding, palm sweating, dumb smile on your face at the thought of him kind of feeling she had with Clayton. He had been her everything until he wasn't or at least until she was no longer that for him.

The last year of her surgical residency at Hopkins had been rough, but was made a little easier when Clayton, who was a year ahead of her, had completed his residency and accepted a job in Texas as head of general surgery. She'd heard about his strides over the years and did her best to avoid looking him up and stalking him on the internet. She eventually found it hard to avoid stories about him and his miraculous surgeries. She was proud of him.

Over the years, she'd participated in many conferences across the country and a few times, she and Clayton would appear at the same location and yet, she was able to avoid direct contact with him. They would see each other and a few times, she caught him smiling her way. She wouldn't return the gesture and so, he kept his distance. Was there still hurt today? No, but he was a constant reminder of the life she thought she was going to have. To have it tank and sink after years of being together, she still questioned what life would have been like if she hadn't hastily ended their relationship. People make mistakes. His was a big one, but was it unforgivable? She was haunted by the idea that they may have been able to survive what he'd done. Now, she would never know. It had been over ten years and they had both moved on to marrying other people.

Looking down at her certificate, she remembered something significant about it that she hadn't thought about in years. Turning it over in her hands, she removed the brown backing and between the certificate and the backing, there was a photo she completely forgot about. It was a picture of her and Clayton on the day he proposed. She thought they were happy. His wandering proved that the happiness she thought they were living together was one-sided. Her ringing cell phone snapped her back into the present knowing she needed to leave the past in the past.

"I promise I'm on my way," Donna said after seeing her sister's face appear on the screen of her phone."

"You better be. I told you I found the perfect outdoor furniture that I know you're going to love, especially since I'm buying it as a housewarming gift to welcome you back to Texas. I can't believe I'm going to have my little sister close enough that I can be at your house in thirty minutes. Can you imagine all the road trips I'm going to take to pick my baby Zoe up! When I told Grace that her cousin Zoe was moving close for many, many sleepovers, that's all she's been talking about. I'm also thinking about all the airfare I will save flying me and Grace back and forth to New York for visits. I love that you're now a road trip away. We always wanted our children to grow up being close like we were when we were their age. With us both having a girl and they're only one year apart, I can't wait for them to be able to see each other all the time. Did the grill come yesterday?" Candace asked.

Donna smacked her own self against the head realizing she forgot to call and thank Candace for the gift of a five-burner gas grill that in fact, did come the day before.

"Yes, and I'm sorry for not calling you last night to tell you it had arrived. I only had yesterday and today off from the hospital. I was attempting to get more of the house unpacked. Having you here has not helped. We seem to find a better use of our time with a bottle of wine. We never get around to actually unpacking anything more than a box or two."

"We finished Zoe's room and that was a major achievement considering I thought Benny agreed to help with that. There is no rush for the rest of it and besides, I'm planning a girl's night out at your house with some friends of yours and a few of mine. We can't wait to say welcome home! What were you doing because I know it wasn't heading out the door? You're always late!"

"I'm in the office here at home. Zoe is always saying when she gets home from school and I've been home all day it never looks like I've unpacked anything. I wanted to show her that I'm making progress. Don't even bring up Benny. He was supposed to put up the shelves in Zoe's room. I ended up hiring the kid of one of the nurses at the hospital. He knocked that out in no time. Benny would have taken days for those eight shelves," she laughed. "I think I'm moving along nicely with this unpacking."

"Well, my niece speaks the truth. I've seen the terror dome that is your home. I tried to help, but you know how that went. What kind of excuses does Benny tossing out now? You let him slide when you stayed in New York and he moved here, but now, he has no room for any excuses when it comes to helping out with Zoe. He lives thirty minutes away like me. I guess he's not going to show and prove as he said he would when you told him you were moving here. He's at that studio day and night. I get that he's remarried and has twins with what's-her-name, but he had Zoe first."

Donna laughed out loud. Candace never held back her dislike for someone.

"Don't call her that. Her name is Alicia and I don't know why you don't like her. What has she done to you?"

"What? I thought were we hating her together. We're not? I've been wasting energy on hating her by myself for no reason?"

"She's not one of my favorite people, but I have no reason to hate her. She's Zoe's stepmother and I need to get along with her and with Benny. Why do I need to hate on her?"

"Other than she was screwing your husband while you were still married to him? I'd say that's a good start."

Donna didn't want to continue to acknowledge that. The woman was now married to her ex and they had to keep the peace for Zoe.

"Benny and I were married but had been separated for over six months at that time; maybe longer than that. You know we lived in a loveless marriage. Him seeing her didn't bother me as deeply as I thought it would. The only thing I care about is how she treats Zoe. I've had that conversation with Benny many times. I let him deal with his wife. He knows when Zoe tells me things that bother me, he doesn't want me handling her so he's on it. He knows better," she proclaimed.

"But we're not hating her though, huh?"

"No, Candace, we are not hating her. We need to keep a united front for my daughter and you know that."

"I guess he's happy now, huh?"

"I don't know. I know he's stressed with the twins. When Zoe is at their house, she says they argue a lot because Benny is never there. The twins are a handful. That's Benny though. I was married to him and I know. Alicia was the clueless one. She thought she was getting the hot television producer when what she got was the workaholic. He's still the same."

"Yeah, but your situation was different. You were going through the motions of being married, but not in love. I'm still sorry you wasted so many years trying to make that work just to say you were making it work. Let me just say that there are lots of hot, sexy guys here in Dallas and in no time, you'll be letting your hair down and hopping on a guy or two!" Candace joked.

"Hopping on a guy or two? Who *are* you? You know how I feel about that. I don't want a bunch of guys in and out of my life and Zoe seeing that. When the time is right and the guy is right, we'll see how it goes."

"No more Keith Lawson's though. He was a clown. I bet he spent more time in front of the mirror than you did. Did he ask you to tell him how good looking he was? I mean, did he request that on the regular?" Candace joked.

When her sister let a yelp escape her lips as she tried to stifle the laugh, Donna wondered why she ever told her about her last boyfriend's obsession with himself. Candace never, ever let that one go.

"I promise, no more guys like that. I happily left him back in New York. You know, good, no great men who are interested in something long-term just don't exist in the current dating environment. Everyone is looking for that right-now kind of connection. I've done that since splitting with Benny and I want more. I deserve more than casual sex with no thoughts of a future."

"And you'll get it because you are a great catch. You're sexy, beautiful, got serious money, a doctor and in better shape than a twenty-year old. I need you to help me work on my weight loss goals. I can't stand that you have time to not only work as a doctor, teach as one, raise Zoe and still have time to work out like a weight trainer. Help me!" Candace yelled.

"I got you. I need to find a good yoga studio and dance class. The dancing works for me and you'll love it. We'll do that together," she offered.

"Finally! See, that's why I'm happy you're back. I

need you closer. I'm going to help you get your dating life back on track. The perfect man is out there and I believe he's living right here in this area," Candace noted.

Just when she expected to hear more, there was silence. Knowing that she and Candace were so close that they would often know what the other was thinking without words being said, she spoke up first.

"You can ask. I know you're dying to. Go ahead," Donna blurted out.

"What will you do when you see him? I say when because now that you are in the same city, there is no way you'll be able to avoid seeing and running into him. You're at two different hospitals, but that doesn't mean a thing. And before you ask, yes, I checked and he is still chief of surgery at Baylor University Medical Center. He's on year three as the chief and he's helped catapult the surgical program into one of the top ones in the country. I heard he also runs a topnotch private practice, too. He's doing amazing work. What will you do?"

"It's funny you would bring that up. I'm standing here at the window in my office with a picture of me and him from back in the day when he proposed. It was in the back of the frame of my certificate from medical school."

"Ten or so years later, are you still hurt and angry over what he did? Let me also add that the brother is still fine as hell. Goodness, I didn't know a man could get more handsome as he aged. Time has been good to him. Don't be mad that I looked him up and have kept up with his career. I've run into him a few times and I don't even live in Dallas. I could tell he wanted to ask about you, but he didn't. I was cordial."

"I'm glad you were. That was a long time ago. No, I'm not angry about that anymore. It's been a long time and I'm over it."

"I wonder if him and that, whew, let me not say the words that I use to describe her, if they are still married and if they've had any other children. Ever wonder about that?"

Donna didn't want to admit that she'd thought the same thing over the years. Shortly after the encounter with him and Michelle, a few months later, she heard that he'd finally moved to Texas and took Michelle with him. Like her, it seems, they had a quickie wedding also. To say she was surprised would be an understatement. A month later, she ran off and married Benny.

"I don't. I did for a long time after he accepted the position here in Dallas and he married her," Donna admitted.

"I was shocked to hear that he'd married her."

"Well, she was pregnant with his baby and I guess he did the right thing. I don't know. That was a long time ago and I've let it go. Let's not talk about that. I need to grab a shower if you want me to meet you at the store on-time."

"Okay, go ahead because I need to get back to Fort Worth before Grace gets out of school. See you in a few."

After ending the call, Donna looked down at the picture in her hand. He's still the greatest love that she'd let slip through her fingers.

When Candace asked her what she would do if she ran into him again, she didn't have an answer that she wanted to share. To herself, she said she would smile and reach out her hand for a handshake. There was no need to harbor ill-will. What's done is done. She also hadn't told Candace that she had looked Clayton up on the internet and marveled at how handsome he still was.

His face beamed across the screen and just like in person, his dark-brown eyes penetrated her very soul. She remembered looking into those eyes and seeing so much love, compassion and passion. Secretly, her heart still melted at the sight of him.

Clayton was tall at six-foot, five-inches. She always loved his close haircut and perfect goatee. From the last picture she saw of him, he still sported the look that worked for him. He'd always been in great shape with perfectly sculpted abs, a six-pack most men admired, muscular legs and hard-rock thighs with the power of a stallion. His smile, with his perfect white teeth, could light up any room. The man was gorgeous and there wasn't a woman who didn't give him a second, third and fourth look. She was one of those women.

If she did run into him, she wouldn't let that show. After all, he belonged to another woman; the same woman who had stolen her hopes and dreams of a life with Clayton, which dashed in what seemed like an instant. She didn't actually know if they were still together. She hadn't dived deep into his personal life, only his life as a surgeon and all the strides he'd made.

Clayton had set out and done exactly what he had planned to do. The only exception had been what he had planned for them as a couple. They would never know if things could have worked out. She had to put him and their past away for good and hope that Dallas was large enough that they didn't have to run into each other with an awkward moment. She could only hope that were possible. She couldn't plan out her reaction if it wasn't. Maybe she wouldn't have to.

Dropping the photo in a nearby box, she once again put off unpacking and raced to shower and dress to get to the store and back in time to pick Zoe up from school. She was done reminiscing about a time in her life that she still wanted to forget about. There went her idea of not caring anymore. It was clear that she still did.

3

The hospital fundraising event, a dinner party, had been a flurry of activity from the moment Clayton had arrived until the moment he was finally able to slip away unnoticed, or so he thought. Accepting the invitation hadn't been on the top of his list of things to do on a Saturday evening after spending the week working several double shifts as chief of surgery. He not only performed his own surgeries at the hospital and at the private practice he ran with his best friend, Sebastian Larsen, a general surgeon, he also oversaw the surgeries of the hospital's interns and residents. His choice, for tonight, would have had him sitting at home catching up on a few basketball games he'd recorded throughout the week. He didn't get much downtime and when he did, he tried to make time where he could relax and unwind or spend quality time with his eleven-year-old daughter, Brooklyn, the light of his life.

As a single parent raising a daughter, being there

as a constant presence in her life was important to him. When he was asked to attend the fundraiser for the hospital, he pushed back complaining of the lack of time he'd spent with Brooklyn throughout the week. The powers that be at the hospital didn't push him too hard, but it was Brooklyn who finally convinced him to go, citing how he never did anything fun that didn't include her.

After leaving work earlier in the day, he'd gone home and changed, not once, but three times after Brooklyn complained about his choice of attire. After an hour of feeling uncomfortable and out of place and overdressed in a black suit and tie, he found an opening to escape when the hospital administrator took to the microphone to thank everyone for coming. When he began his speech to entice people to write big checks so that the hospital could continue to give much needed care to the less fortunate, he made his mad dash for the door.

Finding an exit, he quickened his steps and avoided eye contact with late comers who might ask why he was leaving so early. Getting on the road and heading home, he thought he was in the clear until the ringing of his phone with the familiar ringtone rang out. Sebastian, who he left at the event, had tracked him down. He knew there was no need to ignore the call because Sebastian was that friend who would call and call again until he answered.

Hitting the telephone button on the steering wheel

of his black Mercedes Benz E-Class, he spoke up before his friend could throw a million questions at him.

"I worked double shifts several times this week. I'm exhausted and I was already looking forward to a weekend of doing nothing when I remembered this event was tonight. If you're going to kill me for bailing on it, make it quick," Clayton shared.

"I see a brother has mission impossible level skills. How did you break free so easily? I've been trying to leave since I arrived. Just when I think I'm out, someone drags me back in with a conversation. This thing is a snooze-fest. Teach me your ways sensei," Sebastian joked. "If it wasn't for all of the fine women here tonight, I would come up with a better excuse, but since you left, my appeal with the ladies has raised a few notches. You're my best friend, but around you, when it comes to the ladies, I get a second look, brother," Sebastian kidded.

"Then my leaving is a good thing and gets me off the hook. You can thank me later."

"I was hoping you and me could have picked up a pair of sexy vixens tonight, head out after this thing is over and maybe take them out for a real meal and some dancing. And then who knows, maybe we both could have gotten lucky tonight. There are several women here tonight who don't know about my reputation with the nurses at the hospital, so this would have been my chance with you as my wingman. Tell me you're not really gone, just outside getting some air."

Clayton laughed out loud as he drove through traffic.

"No such luck. In thirty minutes, I'll be home. Sorry for running out, especially on your big plans for the night, but either way, you were going to be solo with any ladies tonight, me or no me."

"When are you going to get back on that horse and have the women clamoring for your attention? You're cramping my style with this all work and no play attitude of late that you have going on."

Clayton shook his head after hearing that same sentiment from most of his friends. He wasn't living the life of a monk. He simply wasn't sharing his personal life with his friends.

"How is my dating or not dating impacting your life? You would still get shot down!"

"Whatever, bro. That's why I needed you with me tonight. I had it all planned out. I just had a very beautiful woman ask me where you were. She saw us talking and when I approached her and a friend who was with her, she was practically breaking her neck to check the room for you. See, that's what I'm talking about. I need you here helping a brother out. As soon as I told her that I thought you had already left, they suddenly felt the need to visit the ladies room. I know they're giving me the slip."

"Ah, so it's possible they've heard about your reputation. I told you about messing around at the hospital where we work. That also extends to our private practice. I don't know all that goes on there since we agreed that as partners in the practice, you would run the day to day, overseeing the other doctors and the staff and outside of the few surgeries I do a week, I handle the administration end of things. I hope you're not making use of that office space like you do at the hospital."

"Of course not. I leave all my fun to the expanse of the hospital. Our private practice is our milk and honey. That's the place that has allowed you and I both to see seven figures for the past two years. I'm not playing any kind of games there. I'm toning my playing at the hospital down, too. Those on-call room antics sometimes call my name," Sebastian joked.

"Yeah, I know. Word gets around. I learned my lesson with doing that a long time ago. Did you learn nothing from my past? I keep telling you that's a bad idea. We've been friends for fifteen years. Remember my life and how my messing around ruined everything?"

"Yeah, but you married that lesson and since you're divorced you can take that lesson and play a new game. I think you should turn around and come back," Sebastian suggested.

"Why? Do you plan on keeping the ladies happy until I get there? No can do. I'm almost home and I see a cold beer and a recorded basketball game in my near future. Brooklyn is over at Reggie and Selena's house for the night and I need to wind down. You're on your own. You can handle it and if not, Dr. Wallace is there; he can be your wingman."

Clayton was thankful for friends like Reggie and Selena Jordan. Until Selena opened up her own private day care a few years ago, she had been the director of the day care center at the hospital where Brooklyn spent her day care years before going to school. Even then, she went to a school nearby that would bring her to the hospital each day. Selena and her husband had become great friends and surrogate parents to Brooklyn. They had their own kids, twin seven-year-old boys and a daughter who was the same age as Brooklyn. She loved hanging out with them as much as they loved having her over. He considered them family.

Wallace was another friend of theirs who wasn't the coolest cat in their group, but he was the most brilliant with a Ph.D. in neuroscience. Everyone called him Wally behind his back, but Clayton never did. They were all glad when they finally were able to convince Wallace that it was okay to wear a shirt without pockets for pens.

"Wally? Aw, why you gotta do a brother like that? Did you see him? He's got on a beige corduroy suit in June and it's hot as hell. I was sweating just looking at him. If that's my only option, I'm good going solo. We still on for Shaba's club opening next weekend?"

Clayton laughed so hard the car swerved.

"Man, you better stop calling Will by that name. Why must you use nicknames in place of people's names? He hates that you call him Shaba! You piss him off every time he hears it. I know you think it's funny, but he doesn't. He's giving us free tickets to the grand opening, so you may not want to give him a reason to throw you out, or even worse. Don't forget he was a contender as a heavy weight boxing competitor a few years ago. One punch and it's all over for you," he chuckled.

"He knows I don't mean no harm when I call him that. His Jamaican accent is so strong. We on or what? I know the honeys will be up in that place. Tickets for the opening have been sold out for weeks."

"Yeah, I wouldn't miss it. If Brooklyn isn't with her mother that weekend, her sitter, Stacy said she was free."

"Brooklyn still trying to convince you that she doesn't need a sitter anymore? Just how fine is your sitter? On a scale, how would she rank? I'm in need of a sitter!"

"Man, you don't have any children, so stop it. Yeah, Brooklyn tries it, but I'm not hearing it. I am not leaving my eleven-year-old daughter at home alone without knowing how late I'll be out. I told her maybe when she's thirteen, but I'm lying. It gives her hope and lets me off the hook from having to tell her no all the time. FYI – I'm not going back, so you're on your own. Just putting that out there before you ask me again."

"Alright, I'm letting you off the hook tonight, but next weekend, no excuses. You said Michelle may be in town or is Brooklyn possibly going to Chicago?"

The last thing he wanted was for his ex-wife to fly into town disrupting his entire life as she has a tendency to do. He also had issues with Brooklyn being in Chicago for a week knowing her mother had no problem leaving her alone in her apartment while she went out on the town. Their divorce was not amicable and the co-parenting could be better, but he was giving it an honest try. He even found the strength to muster up a smile when Michelle was complaining about one thing or another from Brooklyn's hair to her clothes. There was always something. What they have never argued about is him having full custody of their daughter, something he would have fought Michelle to the ends of the earth to have. Thankfully and shamefully, Michelle didn't fight him for custody. She didn't even put up a front to make it look like she cared where Brooklyn lived. He offered shared custody and she didn't want that, though he never told Brooklyn that. He didn't want her to think that her mother didn't want or love her.

"At first she wanted Brooklyn to go to Chicago for two weeks with school over for the year. Then she called and said a week because she had something that was going to come up during the second week. The latest is she is going to fly here for a few days and hang out with Brooklyn and then fly off to someplace that I don't care about. I don't know. We'll see if she even shows up."

"I can see why you have regrets over messing around where you work. I don't know if marrying her was the answer because you got her pregnant but hey, you're a better man than me. Do you ever think about her? You know who."

Clayton knew exactly who he was talking about. Anytime he talked to any friends from Johns Hopkins, he thought about her. He couldn't help but do that. There had been many times over the past twelve years that he'd thought about her.

"If there was ever a learning opportunity for no playing at work, you should look to my history and act accordingly and not how you usually do. I really messed that up. Donna was perfect. I didn't appreciate what I had with her."

"Those days of being at Johns Hopkins together were the best times. Baltimore has all that great food and even sexier women. I guess coming back home to Dallas, your hometown, to work was your way of starting over. I'm just glad you hired me and gave me a chance to start out fresh here."

"It was and besides, before my parents retired to St. Petersburg, Florida two years ago, Brooklyn got to be around them a lot. She's going to spend a few weeks with them right before school starts back up in August."

"Good luck with Michelle. I know what it's like when she visits and then leaves and Brooklyn has to be reprogrammed from her mother's outlandish idea of how her daughter should have more independence."

"She doesn't get that an eleven-year-old girl doesn't need the freedom to do whatever she wants. Trust, I'm already preparing for her visit and Brooklyn is becoming immune to Michelle's dropping in and out of her life on a whim. Either way, that weekend, I'm good to hang out and I promise to not give you the slip like I did tonight. I'm off the rest of the weekend, so I'll see you Monday at the hospital," Clayton said.

"I've got three surgeries scheduled for Monday. I'll try and catch you in between or at the surgical board," Sebastian explained.

Clayton nodded. Mondays were always the most interesting day of the week at the hospital. It was the day that the surgeons got together in one room to discuss what went well and what didn't go so well as far as surgeries from the week before. He led those sessions and was glad they could be used as a learning opportunity for everyone, including him.

"Cool."

"Listen, Clay, I have something I want to bring up that happened right after you left. I'm not sure you will find that news good or bad, but here it goes. There were several doctors talking and I joined in on the discussion regarding other Dallas hospitals and one in particular would have been of interest to you. It's about a new doctor at one in particular. I think you would want to know about this before you're surprised with it one day."

"You are long-winded. Spill it, Sebastian," Clayton

pressured.

"Okay. The main reason I went looking for you was that I was talking to a few doctors from Children's Health Systems of Texas in Dallas and they were talking about their new Pediatric Surgeon and research coordinator and all of the great research and strides she is making in dealing with cancer in children."

"Okay," Clayton shared while on the verge of losing his patience. "Still long-winded," he stated.

"Right, right. Well, it's Donna."

Clayton's back stiffened as the car suddenly swerved a little to the left. The car in that lane honked at him and he waved his apologies. His Donna? Not being presumptuous, he waited and then edged Sebastian on for more.

"Donna? Donna who?"

"Donna Johnson, well, Donna Spencer is her name now, but yeah, that Donna. I wasn't sure, so after hearing about her profession and knowing that's what she'd always said she wanted to devote her time to, I took out my phone and pulled up the hospital website. I found her in the staff listing. She's been there about a month now, maybe a little longer, I'm not sure. I can confirm that it's her. The picture is recent and let me just say that she is more beautiful than ever. I mean, she is drop-dead, out of this world stunning and glamorous. She's the beauty you once loved and she's here in Dallas; a stone's throw away from you after all these years. Can you believe that? I wasn't sure you knew. I assumed you didn't since you haven't said anything to me."

Clayton wasn't sure he was hearing Sebastian right. He'd just been thinking about Donna and now he's hearing that she's in Dallas.

"What? Donna is here in Dallas working? You're sure?" he asked.

He could feel his heart rate increase as he shifted uncomfortably in his seat. He had the windows down with his favorite Mary J. Blige songs playing in rotation. His thoughts shifted to the love that he let get away. He had to see and know for himself. Seeing an empty parking spot a few blocks from his own home, he couldn't wait. He pulled out of traffic into the spot and grabbed his iPad from the passenger seat. With fingers that seemed to move with the speed of light, he pulled up the hospital website just as Sebastian said he had done and within seconds, he found her. On the screen looking back at him was the one and only woman he'd ever loved; the woman he once wanted to spend an eternity with if in his past, he'd listened more to the head on top of his body instead of the one in his pants. He could hear Sebastian talking, but didn't understand any of the words coming out of his mouth. Clayton's only focus was on the incredibly beautiful woman who appeared to be staring back at him; that's just what photos do.

It was her eyes. He looked at them and then at everything else about her in the photo. Sebastian was right; Donna was even more beautiful than he remembered. Instead of her hair being cut short in a mass of curls, it was now long and flowing around her shoulders with various hues from brown to gold. He knew she could rock any style, but this one did give her a glamourous look and he loved it. She had on light makeup in hues of gold and what looked to be a few shades of beige around her eyes and on her lips. His eyes locked on her perfectly shaped lips, one's he still missed kissing and loving on. She was wearing her hospital coat in one photo with her name visible. Sebastian was right, her last name was no longer Johnson; it was Spencer. She was married. That realization caused his heart to sink. He didn't know why, other than it pained him to think of someone else making her happy the way he always wanted to. In another photo, one that was a full body shot of her, he noticed how sexy she truly was. She was in a dark orange, form fitting dress, which held on to her curves perfectly. He looked down to her manicured nails and noticed that her wedding ring finger was empty; there was no ring. Perhaps she was divorced like him?

Was he hyperventilating with excitement? She was in Dallas and so was he. Had she thought about him recently? She had to know that he was still in Dallas. Was she happy? From her radiant smile, she looked happy.

"Clay? Did you hear me? Are you listening?" Sebastian screamed through the phone, snapping

Clayton out of the nostalgic moment.

"Yeah, yeah, I hear you. Look, I'll call you tomorrow."

"Cool. Look, before you go, I forgot to check with you about the beach house in Galveston. Are you still planning on a week away this summer? I know you try to get there several times a year. You said you wanted to have a few of us come down this summer and I'm trying to plan my week. Any week in mind?" Sebastian asked.

Clayton smiled when he thought about his favorite home away from home. A year ago, he purchased a nice beachfront four-bedroom, five-bath house right on the beach in Galveston. There were times he and Brooklyn took the long drive on a Friday for the weekend when he could get that kind of time off. This summer, he was planning on several weeks on the beach, learning to enjoy life more and not work as much. Besides, he promised Brooklyn some extra time this summer on the beach.

"I've already put in for a few weeks this summer, two single weeks and then two weeks together at the end of the summer, right before Brooklyn goes back to school. You know my child is a fish when it comes to water and I promised her. I'll text you the week I'm thinking about. I need to tell Patrick too, so that he and Marcelle can come down. Reggie and Selena will need to plan early too for them and the kids to come down. I know they take vacations as a family around that time of year. Are you bringing a date or coming down solo?" Clayton asked.

"I'm definitely going to bring a date. I have a friend I'd like to bring."

"Okay, what kind of friend is this? Any future in it?"

"I don't know. You know me, I play it by ear. She does have two kids who like me and I like them. She doesn't get to go away much as a single parent and I think she'd fit in with our group."

"Wait? Are you talking about Nora?"

"Yes. You like her, right?"

Clayton loved her for Sebastian. She was the only woman he'd ever known Sebastian to date that he could see him with long-term. She ran a local and very successful event planning business. He'd actually been to an event or two that she had planned and he remember how well they had turned out.

"You know I like her. I think that she is perfect for you. I also know that you're afraid that you really like her too. That's why you continue to serial date and always turn back to her."

"She is kind of great. You're good if I bring her and her kids? She's got a son and a daughter and both are around Brooklyn's age."

"That would be perfect. It should be a good week for us all."

"Are you bringing a date?" Sebastian asked. "Valerie perhaps?" he added.

"I don't know. We're not really seeing each other like that – at least not enough for a full week away together. She's cool and all, but I don't know if I want to give her the idea that we're more than friends who have sex every now and then. It's good sex – I mean it's really great sex, but we're not in that, going away with groups of friends, kind of relationship. She whizzes in and out of town, so I don't know if her schedule will allow it, anyway. I'll see."

"Cool. I'm going to let you go and have your quiet time. Besides, I brought up Donna and I know you want to spend some time thinking about her and checking her out the minute we hang up. I won't joke you on that. Catch you next week!" Sebastian yelled.

"Later, bro."

Just like that, Sebastian was gone and Clayton's head once again was filled with Donna. He stared at her photo remember happier times. Any spare time they had where their schedules matched, they would find time to squeeze in a date night. When they lived in Maryland, they loved venturing down to the Inner Harbor or taking a quick drive to Washington, D.C., to take in a museum. One of their favorite places to go was to M Street in Georgetown where they walked the streets like everyone else and stopped into the various restaurants for delicious foods. Those were good times and it was then that he knew she was the one for him. He hadn't set out to be the kind of guy who hurts a woman, who cheats on a woman he loved, but he did turn into that guy.

He thought he knew the plan for his life from back when he was a young boy. He always wanted to be a doctor. He graduated valedictorian of his high school class. He was in the top two percent, grade point average wise in undergraduate school, even graduating a semester early. Medical school came easy for him and he was the best of the best as an intern and during his residency. Instructors and mentors filled his head with praise and accolades. He was at the top when it came to his profession and to top all of that off, he had fallen in love with Donna.

They were all set to get married and live an incredible life as doctors. He had become so full of himself that he took Donna's love for granted by sneaking around with other women. One woman here and there became several more women. That then turned into women at the hospital. That became his downfall. He played where he worked. Those were fun times and when he came across a willing participant and an empty room, he went with the desires of his body instead of the sensibility of his heart and mind. He was following what he'd seen other doctors doing for years. Other than Brooklyn, things hadn't turned out well for him.

Pulling back out into traffic, the rest of his ride home was all about Donna. The second he saw her picture, one thing rang true for him; after all of these years, he was still in love with her; with the woman he knew back them. He wondered what she was like now besides being more beautiful than ever. His feelings for her never waned, even throughout his tumultuous marriage to Michelle, which hadn't lasted long. He tried to do the right thing by marrying her when what he should have done was focused on being a good father. He fixed that the day he filed for divorce and full custody. He was happy, but his mind still turned to how happy he could have been with what should have been.

4

Donna was happy she was out of state at a medical conference and not close enough to her ex to give him the read she needed to lay on him in person.

"Benny Spencer!" she yelled into the phone. Her patience for dealing with him was gone.

"Okay, can you tone it done a little," he exclaimed in response to her screaming his name through the phone.

"I could, but why would I? Zoe called and said she's at your parents' house instead of with you at your house where we agreed she would be. Before I left to travel out of town, that was our understanding. What is it this time?"

"Work is crazy," he tried to explain.

"School let out yesterday and the last conversation I had with you was that you were picking her up to stay with you this week while I'm away speaking at a conference. This was planned when I first moved to Dallas. She called to tell me that you, instead, dropped her off with her grandparents with a promise from you to stop by and see her every day. She's not someone you can pick and choose if you'll have time for her; she's our daughter who lives a lot closer to you now and yet, she barely sees you. This is one week; one week and you've already failed."

Donna tried to work with Benny on co-parenting, but there were times like now, when she lost her cool when he didn't make Zoe a priority. She thought she would be able to hold back her anger but the minute she heard his voice, she couldn't help the rage that accompanied her words. They often disagreed on just about everything when it came to their shared custody of their only child and at nine years old, Zoe needed more than a sometime father.

"Look, I hear you but you know Alicia just had twins and she's still adjusting to their schedule. I have a busy week at work on two new shows I'm producing for the studio and both are requiring more of my time than I thought they would. Besides, I forgot that Zoe was coming this week."

Donna sighed out her frustration to hear that Benny somehow forgot about his obligation to his only daughter.

"You say that all the time, Benny. The excuse of Alicia and the twins has gotten really old. The twins are ten months old now and she's not doing it alone; she has you. Women have kids every day. You can't decide to claim Zoe as an active member of your household during the year when you get to claim her on your taxes. She is your daughter every day of every year, so do better."

"You are just never happy. I agree to pick her up a week earlier than she is scheduled to come here and you still complain. She'll be with my parents for a few days while I take care of some business. I didn't want Alicia complaining about me leaving all three kids for her to look after. Cut me some slack."

"You know what, I usually cut you slack. I do it all the time. I do it when she's all packed to join you for your weekend and you forget to come and get her as if she's an afterthought and not your daughter. I cut you slack when she has an event and you don't show up after promising her that you would. I cut you all kinds of slack, so don't act like you have a reason to be upset here. I always appreciate when I have a speaking engagement and you offer to help out even when it's not your weekend. All I'm asking is that you not forget about her when you've made a commitment. I'm not asking for me, I'm asking for her. You complained when we lived in New York and you had to fly in to pick her up for your visits or fly with her back to New York. I moved closer so that you could have a better, ongoing relationship with her."

"I know. I hadn't planned things out well," he admitted.

"You're right; you didn't. She has her first day of camp on Monday and she was looking forward to bragging about you going with her for the few hours in the morning. They asked the parents to be there to learn more about what the camp is about. When we discussed this trip I'm on, you told me you understood how important my research work is and that you were looking forward to having that time with her. I never would have committed to being on the agenda if I had known you wouldn't do what you promised. I could have asked for a change in my presentation or I could have sent her to my sister. We need to work together here. I know how much she loves your parents and being with them for a week is no problem for her nor is it for me. I still love them very much. I appreciate how much they love Zoe and would do anything for her. She's not saying it, but she really wanted you to go with her. You should have just told me is all I'm saying."

Donna waited for Benny to come back with a retort to explain himself. She prepared herself for his usual selfish response that he's balancing a lot. When she heard him exhale loudly, she didn't know what to expect.

"I hear you Donna and I'm sorry for disappointing Zoe yet again. She shouldn't have to feel like she's second fiddle to anything in my life. It's just been crazy with Alicia complaining all the time about how the twins are a handful and they are. Those boys are giving her a time now that they are walking. I didn't want Zoe there to hear Alicia complain for a week. I thought her being with my parents would be better for her. She loves them and they enjoy having her, especially now that you've moved to Dallas. When I mentioned it to my mom, she was so excited to have Zoe for this time. My dad started making lists of snacks to buy and they even added some of the cable channels she loves to watch that they don't usually have. I thought it would be good for her. I'm sorry if you think it wasn't."

Now she felt bad. Perhaps it was the stress of the conference that had her on edge more than usual. Though her divorce from him was a bad time for both of them, it had been years ago and they were in a better place. She needed to lay off, remembering that she was out of town. She was in no position to complain about what he wasn't doing when he made a way that she knew made Zoe happy. She loved her grandparents, G-Pop and Gammy, her names for them.

"Look, I'm sorry. I don't mean to fuss. It's the stress of this week's conference and the fact that I'm missing Zoe's last day of school and first week of camp next week. Her not having me or you at camp really bothered me, though your parents would be great stand-ins."

"Don't worry about it. Look, I'll make some changes and go with her for her first day of camp. If you're really concerned about her being with my parents, I'll bring her to my house and deal with Alicia. My home is Zoe's home too. I really was looking out for her because Alicia has been on a rampage lately. Listen, when camp is over, I was thinking of taking some time off. Alicia and I were going to take a trip to Florida, probably Miami for a week. It's not during my time with Zoe, but I'm hoping you'll let her come along. I've been looking into it. I could email you the details. Let me know if that works."

"I'm sure it will be fine. I would like the details, especially the dates. Does she know?"

"I haven't said anything yet. I didn't know if you had plans for the rest of the summer. You usually take her someplace for a few weeks."

"I always make plans, but I can work around your schedule this summer. Zoe would love that time away with you and Alicia. Since we just moved back to the area, I have a lot of unpacking and settling into the house to get done which will take me most of the summer anyway. Send me what you have on the Miami trip, but we don't need to talk about if she can go or not; she can definitely go. She'll love that."

"Yeah, she loves the beach. I remember when she was a baby and how much she loved the water."

"She still does. If you can make Monday, that would make her happy. Please try and do so. All I ask is you keep me in the loop. I'm going to see if Candace can go, just as a backup. Let's communicate better. I shouldn't have to hear about a change like her not staying with you, from her. I should hear that from you."

"Noted. I'll give her a call this evening. Don't say anything yet in case I can't make a change, but I will try," Benny said.

"Do better Benny. That's all I ask is for you to do better. She loves you. I know having twins is a lot to take on, but don't push Zoe to the side because it's easier. You have to make it work with all three of your children," she said.

"You're right. Have a good speech. I'll see you when you get back and I drop her off in a week. I may be able to pick her up next Friday. My flight comes in early. If there are no delays, I'll get her and text you early enough."

After the conversation ended, Donna called Zoe who she knew was waiting on her phone call. They had been speaking earlier and were interrupted by a call from her assistant who was back in her office at the Children's Medical Center Dallas, a nationally ranked pediatric acute care teaching hospital. Though she was away, she had a special case of a child who was in crisis and could be in need of a kidney soon. It was the first case assigned to her by the hospital once she arrived in town. She had just enough time to talk to Zoe and finish their conversation before she had to get ready for her Friday night speech, the opening night of the conference she was attending in New York.

"Zoe, I just spoke with your father about the change in you staying with him and Alicia."

"Mommy, I told you I was fine. Being with G-Pop and Gammy is fine. I love it at their house and there are no screaming babies. The last time I stayed with dad and Alicia, the babies kept me up all night. I ended up tired the whole weekend."

"I know you're fine with your grandparents. That's not the issue here. If he was going to be too busy, which he knew and didn't say, all he had to do was say so and I could have made other arrangements for you. You have camp on Monday and it's your first day. Did you ask your grandfather about that? I don't want you to miss anything."

"G-Pop already knows and so does Gammy. Dad told them and they promise to make sure I get to camp on time and will pick me up every day. You really need to chill, mommy. I'm fine and guess what? Gammy bought me a new bedroom set for their house. I have a bigger bed and everything. She said I was getting to be a big girl and big girls needed a bigger bed. It's not a twin bed, it's a full size like I have at home. She even bought me a desk that matches the bed."

"Oh, that sounds pretty. Make sure you thank her for you and for me. Send me lots of pictures. I'm sorry I'm missing your first week of camp. I bet you'll have so much fun that you won't even miss me. I have a sad face, even though you can't see it."

"I already miss you and I can't wait for you to get back. Are we still going to that craft class you signed us up for? I want to ask dad to buy me some equipment to make crafts at home, but I want to be able to tell him about the classes first so that he can see how important it is that I have the stuff to make my own crafts."

"I wouldn't miss it at all. I always look forward to more time for us to spend together. You're getting so big and soon, you'll be ten years old. Time is moving too fast for me," Donna laughed.

"We spend a lot of time together, mom. I mean, like, every single day, except when you have to travel."

"I know and I wish you had this week with your father."

"Yeah, he's not really good at the bonding thing and now with the twins, he has even less time. It's not because he spends a lot of time with them either, at least not when I'm around. He usually picks me up, drops me off at the house and is gone until after I'm in bed. He's already out of the house when I get up in the morning. I can't wait until I'm old enough to stay home alone."

"I'm not looking forward to that at all. That means I have to worry more. Then I'll have to make some changes in my travel for work."

"Mommy, I love you, but you really need to get a life."

"I do have a life; it's you."

"What about a boyfriend?"

"Zoe!"

"Well, you're always saying I can talk to you about anything and this is one of those anything times. You didn't mean that?" she asked.

Donna knew she was caught in that between a rock and a hard place zone. She has always drilled into her only child that no topic was off the table; they could talk about anything. She knew it was too late to change the parameters of that notion. She loved their open and honest dialogue. There were times that she may have opened a can of worms on their free dialogue.

"I did and you can talk to me about anything, but I actually meant anything that involves you, not my personal life."

"Your personal life does involve me. I'm getting older mom. I'm almost ten and that's practically a teenager."

"No, it isn't," Donna countered immediately.

"Casey's mom has a new boyfriend and she likes him. She said he really treats her mom nice and they do a lot of fun stuff together; even that adult stuff you hate to talk to me about."

"Zoe Monet Spencer!"

"Ugh, okay mom. I'm sorry."

"You know I like Casey, but she's twelve and her mother exposes her to too much."

Donna was happy they left Casey back in New York. She only had to worry about the girls chatting on the phone.

"I got it. Your personal life, including your sex life is none of my business. Do you have a sex life?"

Donna covered her mouth and laughed low so that Zoe couldn't hear her. She blames herself for that *'in your face'* kind of way her nine-year-old talks. When she began having *'the talks'* with Zoe, she had no idea it would lead to crossing into her own life.

"Child, I did not talk to you about sex and relationships for you to try and apply them to me; I'm your mother and that's off limits. We talk about those things to prepare you for what's coming your way, hopefully with a lot more years in-between now and then. You need not worry about me and what I do when it comes to that."

"I'm not. It's just talk with Casey; that's all."

"Child of mine, where are you getting this stuff? Don't make me have to bar you from talking to Casey."

"Um."

"I'm waiting? When are you discussing my personal life and with whom?"

Donna was bothered that Zoe was actually having grown-up conversations outside of their chats.

"Mom, it's not like that."

"Why were you discussing me? Talk about stuff you enjoy doing."

"We didn't talk about you. It wasn't Casey."

Dumbfounded, Donna looked at her phone in confusion before placing it back up to her ear.

"Then who was it?"

"Dad and Alicia. Please, don't tell them. I don't want to get in any trouble."

Donna almost dropped her phone.

"Okay, first of all, why would you get in any trouble and why were they talking about me?"

"Well, a few weeks ago when I was at their house

for dad's weekend with me, Alicia said she didn't know it was his weekend because he made plans to be away. She was mad that she would have the twins and me to look after. She thought you sent me to them because you had a new man in your life or something like that. Dad said it was his weekend and even if it wasn't, I wouldn't be with them because you were with some man because you don't have a man. Please don't be mad. I hate when you and dad fight."

Donna gasped in horror. How dare Alicia or Benny make any comments about her personal life, which was none of their business. She was pissed, but she wouldn't take it out on Zoe, nor would she violate their circle of trust by confronting Benny. She just wanted to know what was said. They needed to be more careful in what they say around Zoe. She would bring that up with him.

"I'm not mad and never would I be mad at you for something they said. Let me just say this, whether I date, have a boyfriend or whatever, it's none of their business. They shouldn't have been discussing it whether you were there in ear-range or not. It's an inappropriate discussion to have."

"Dad is always talking to his friends about being happy, especially when Alicia isn't around, like when we're in his car and he's on the phone."

"I want you to listen to me carefully here. Don't you spend time worrying about my happiness, your father's happiness or Alicia's happiness. You need to focus on being nine, almost ten and having the time of your life in camp this summer. I love my life, I'm happy and I love you more than anything in this world. I need to run to my presentation, but I will call you when I get back to my hotel room. Thank your grandparents for me and for your new bedroom set. I love you, Zoe. More than anything else, make sure you know that I love you very much."

"I know, mommy. I love you too. I'll take pictures of my new room."

"Good. I can't wait to get them. Talk to you tonight."

Donna sat on the bed. She wondered when did Zoe get to be so mature? She was also mind-numbing angry at Benny for minding her business. What was he trying to insinuate by saying he knew she didn't have a man? Just because he wasn't a good husband didn't mean there wasn't a better man out there for her.

Brushing off all thoughts of her ex-husband and their marriage that never should have been, she checked herself out in the mirror and prepared to make her presentation on the care of infants and children with life-impairing or life-threatening congenital and acquired disorders.

Talking to Zoe reminded her that she would love to have more time to focus on something other than work. She couldn't blame her life as a mother because unlike when Zoe was younger and less independent, she did have more time to have a personal life. Zoe was involved in many activities from sports to dance and now to crafting, something she loved doing. Where there was a class that she could get her in to improve on the things she loved, there was the opportunity for her to have more time to have more enjoyment. Her issue was, she just didn't.

Checking the time, she knew now wasn't the moment for her to dive into all the ways she could have more fun in her life. She had someplace to be.

Grabbing what she needed, she again checked her attire. Her black pencil skirt and suit jacket over a crisp pink satin shirt complimented her soft pink makeup of eyeshadow and lipstick. Little touches of jewelry accented her look well and her favorite black and pink stilettos were exactly what she needed. Her long curly hair only needed a quick fluff with her hands and she was good to go. With her mind off of family and on business, she was ready.

5

"Here you are. I've been looking all over for you."

Clayton turned his head to see Sebastian grab the seat next to him in the surgical observation room.

"Hey, what's up?" he asked.

"I thought you were going to observe an intern in action in operating room three after your surgery. I finally found you here. What's below?" Sebastian observed.

"Patrick is doing a heart bypass surgery and I wanted to observe."

"Ah, your second-best friend who also happens to be the number one cardio god in the country," Sebastian boasted.

"Hey, he's as much of a perfect friend as you are, so don't hate," Clayton grinned. "You're an ortho god and an attending. We're three brothers with a pact to lead the way for other brothers to see that it's possible to start on this path and stay on top. Do you know how rare it is to have a chief of surgery who is African

American and the two top attendings, you, an orthopedic surgeon and Patrick, an attending who is a cardiothoracic surgeon? What do you have today?" Clayton asked.

"I'm about to do a surgical consult. I'm going to try and make sure a track star will get to shine again after a tragic car accident shattered both of his legs. How did your surgery go this morning?"

"It was postponed. The patient has a fever which we need to get under control before I operate. I got the call early this morning before I left the house to drop Brooklyn off for her first day of summer camp. That gave me a chance to check out her class without having to rush off. When I told her I was going to watch the opening program, she was so excited."

"Ah, summer camp time."

"Yeah. She was worried that she wouldn't make any friends. She was nervous that no one would like her. She's at a camp that's a little out of the way from where we live, so she wasn't sure she would know anyone there. I observed for about thirty minutes and she had already found friends. I looked her way as I was leaving and they were talking a mile a minute. When I left, she waved, smiled and then gave me the thumbs up. I live to see her happy."

"That's because you were meant to be a father. I see that now. I know it wasn't the way you were planning, but I know you wouldn't change anything if it meant you wouldn't have Brooklyn."

Clayton thought about those words and Donna's face came to mind.

"I could easily say I would change things and not have hurt Donna, but that may have meant that I wouldn't have my little girl. I can't have that. Brooklyn was unexpected but the best gift of life I could have ever received, even if her mother is, well, who she is."

"Have you heard from her yet? She still coming to hang with Brooklyn this weekend?" Sebastian asked.

"She called me last night to ask me to apologize to Brooklyn for her because she can't make it. She has some kind of last-minute thing come up. If she came to Dallas, it would only be for a few hours. I told her to not worry about that. A few hours of her time is torture for Brooklyn. I texted her sitter and she's still available on Friday. Brooklyn will be fine. Michelle gave me another weekend that works better for her. Luckily, I never told Brooklyn she was coming, so I don't have to disappoint her with the news that yet again, her mother doesn't have time. It wasn't as much of a problem when she was very little, but at her age, she's starting to really miss not having her mother around more often."

"Brookie will be fine because she has you. Man, how do you do it? Chief of surgery with a crazy schedule and you run around behind my favorite eleven-year-old?"

"The stars are aligned in my favor I guess."

"Now, if we can just get your personal life back on track, we're good," Sebastian whispered so that others in the observation room couldn't hear him.

"There is nothing wrong with my personal life."

"Oh, yes there is. If I didn't have this consult, I'd run down all the ways you're slipping, man. Friday night will be a blaze of a night. I know there will be a bunch of beautiful women at the grand opening."

Clayton shook his head and sighed. If he wasn't planning on supporting another one of his friends who was opening up his first club, he would back out.

"I'm there and looking forward to it."

"Yes!" Sebastian cheered drawing the attention of everyone.

"Really?" Clayton humorously chastised.

"Sorry. Do you have any idea of the kind of trouble we can get into on Friday? I know I call him Shaba, but Will happens to know some of the hottest women in the world, especially celebrities like actresses, models, singers. He did that commercial with those models and now he calls them all friends. I hear that a bunch of them are coming to the opening. Did you think any more about Donna after we talked a few days ago?"

Clayton didn't even attempt to hesitate with his response.

"She's all I've been thinking about."

"Do you know if she's still married? Maybe she's divorced like you are and the two of you can get a second chance."

"Second chance? Who said anything about that?" Clayton asked defensively.

"Whoa, no need to take my head off. I remember what you were like after everything went down back at Hopkins. Are you telling me that if there was any chance for you to have that magic back with her or with any woman, you wouldn't take it? I get it that you're particular about the women you expose Brooklyn to, but seriously, have you seen pictures of Donna Johnson? I know you looked her up. Don't even try to deny it. I know you."

"Yeah, I did and she's beautiful. Her last name isn't Johnson, it's Spencer."

"Well, Michelle still has your last name and you're divorced."

"Sebastian, let it go. I thought you had a consult to get to," Clayton said standing as his phone vibrated on his hip. Checking it, he made a dash for the door.

"Catch you later?" Sebastian asked behind him.

"Yeah. There's an emergency with my patient. I've got a busy week. If we don't connect much, I'll see you Friday night."

"Bet!"

Clayton rushed toward the surgical wing, grateful that he was able to escape further conversation about Donna. He had yet to take it all in that they were once again in the same town. He needed time to think before his friends began bombarding him with questions. Even Patrick, who had heard that Donna was now at a nearby hospital, had called him the night before to pick his brain on his response to Donna. He brushed him off too. His work as a doctor was more important than anything else, including the woman who'd stolen every second of every dream he'd had the past few nights. Truth be told, he couldn't wait to see her again in the flesh. He just wasn't sure she would feel the same way.

**

Donna paced and paced some more as she waited to hear from Zoe. When she checked the time, she knew that Zoe should be done for the day. She was still kicking herself that she had to travel the same week that Zoe would be starting summer camp. At least they could face time and she could hear all about her first day, if she would just call. She would give her a few more minutes and then she'd call her. Before her next thought, her phone pinged and she leaped for it where it sat on the small desk chair in her hotel room.

"Hey, baby!" she shouted excitedly.

"Hey to you too, though I'm not sure why you're calling me baby," Candace exclaimed.

"Oh, I thought you were Zoe. I didn't look at the phone before answering. I'm waiting to hear about her first day of camp."

"I can tell you that she had a wonderful time. I got there just as Benny was dropping her off this morning. He had to drop her off early because of the morning show he's producing, but hey, he came through."

"Benny did the drop off? I thought her grandfather was dropping her off because he couldn't make it."

"I was as shocked as you are, but he came through.

After you sent me a text asking if I could make it, I moved some things around, especially with Grace at sleep away camp. He did and he hung around for the opening program and long enough to make Zoe happy. She kept turning around to wave at him. He was happy he made the time too. I didn't hang around long, but I did give her a big hug and wished her a great first day. She was nervous, but I encouraged her with the same kind of wisdom I bestow upon you on a regular basis."

"Sis, thanks for always having my back."

"See? This is the first of many great things I can now help you out with when it comes to Zoe now that you're closer. You know if you need me, all you have to do is ask. Speaking of asking, I'm calling to see if you want to hang out on Friday night. I know it's the day you travel back home, but a friend told me about this new club that's opening. She was able to score us tickets. According to her, that wasn't easy to do considering the waitlist is a mile long. This can be your initiation back onto the scene. Besides, you could use a fun night."

"Friday? That will be my first day home and I want to spend it with Zoe."

"I hear you, but this night is going to be epic and I know you could use some adult fun for a change. You said the hospital gave you the entire weekend off because you're away this week at the conference representing them. You and Zoe will have the rest of the weekend for girl stuff. Come on. It will be fun and I won't bother you for the rest of the weekend. Plus, Grace comes back next week and I won't have the next weekend free. Please?"

Donna thought about it and knew that she could use a night out. Usually, if she had evenings and weekends free, she spent it with Zoe. Adult company and a few adult drinks were something she could really use.

"Okay, that actually sounds good."

"Great. Let me mention up front that one of my friends going with us is a guy and his name is Lance. I think you'll like him. I have a feeling the two of you will have a lot in common. Before you chop my head off, he's coming as just another friend, but if you like him, go for it. He's single, owns a construction company, no kids and he's good looking."

Donna sighed loudly.

"I should have known you had some ulterior motive planned. Why can't you ever just come at me straight? You could and should have led with that. I don't need or want to be set up with a guy."

"Really? Are you sure about that? I remember our conversations about your New York dating life and from what I heard, that part of your life leaves a lot to be desired. I want you to be happy."

"I am happy."

"Okay, let me be clearer. Happy and in love. Don't you miss that?"

She dared not admit to that or Candace would

spend her days and nights trying to play matchmaker.

"Stop it. I don't need you to find me a man. When the right one comes along, I'll know it."

"Okay. I hear you. Lance will be fun if nothing else. Maybe he's a one-night-stand kind of guy."

"So, you're worried about my love life or my sex life? I'm not sure what your true angle is here, but you're just as single as I am. Find your own man or one-night-stand!" Donna quipped.

"We'll talk about that when we have the ladies night out at your house. I've got my eye on someone and I think it may be getting kind of serious. More later. I wanted to make sure you would plan for Friday night in case you wanted to check Benny's availability."

"I may let her stay an additional night with my ex-in-laws. She's staying with them instead of Benny this week. I'll call them shortly."

"Why isn't she with him? I thought that was the plan?"

"It was. Alicia finds it hard to juggle three kids. According to Zoe, her father takes that time to escape them all. I'll work something out."

"You know, mom and dad keep asking me to push you for Zoe to visit with them. School is out. You should take advantage of that gift before they start vacationing. Grace is there all the time."

"I know that I should. With dad still moving pretty slow after his surgery, I didn't want to put too much pressure on him to entertain her like he wants too. I wanted to allow a little extra time for healing."

"Please! Can you believe they went line dancing last weekend? The seniors center where mom goes to knit and craft has line dancing twice a month. He's fine."

"I'll call and make plans. I want to get them more time with her since we've lived away for so long."

"Good idea. You have many choices for Friday, so no excuses. Wear something cute, sexy and very tight. That perfect body of yours was made for those little, sexy dresses."

Donna smiled. She missed going out and letting her hair down. A cute, little sexy dress sounds perfect.

"I've got something in mind."

"I can't wait. We're going to have so much fun. I forgot to tell you that mom mentioned to me that she hasn't seen your new house yet. I can't believe you haven't had her over. She knows I've been several times. Maybe invite them for dinner?"

Donna knew she was being a terrible daughter. She wanted her house all setup before inviting her mother over.

"Before I've finished unpacking my house? No way. Mom would be there until every room was unpacked with everything put away. She would then go through and clean every room from top to bottom like she's the maid. You know how she is. I need the house to be all setup the way I want because if not, and mom gets her hands on my house, it will be setup the way she wants.

I'll call her this week."

"I know that's right. After my divorce from Terry two years ago,

I decided to do some re-decorating and mom took total control. I had to send Grace to her father's house to give her a reprieve from mom telling her how her room should be. Grace had her own ideas. That was a wild time, but I survived and so will you."

Donna laughed.

"We'll see. How is Terry? You guys get along better divorced?"

"Much better. I mean, you have no idea how much better, but that's a discussion for another time. I'm weighing some stuff."

"He's still enjoying coaching pro-football?" Donna asked.

"He is and with the pre-season about to start, he wants to get in as much time with Grace as he can. He came over to take Grace to her sleepaway camp. He's looking really good these days."

"Wait! Are you feigning for your ex? Tell me it's true!" Donna asked.

"Can we focus on you and not me."

"I was sad to hear about your split. Look at us both, divorced."

"I still think there is hope for you, though," Candace asserted.

"What?"

Donna knew what was coming.

"Um, can we stop at Baylor one day soon and say hello to Clayton?"

Donna chuckled.

"You just don't stop, do you? No, we are not stopping by Baylor. Don't let me hear that you've done that on your own. Clayton is my past. I'm sure his wife wouldn't like me popping up in his life."

"Poot to her. I'm still not over the conniving way in which she trapped him. I still think he's a great guy, I always have."

"Let's leave my past in the past. Can we agree to that?" Donna pleaded.

"I hear you. No more talk about Clayton unless you bring it up."

"Cool. I need to run so that I can call Zoe. I thought she would have called me by now. I have an evening session I'm speaking at and I want to get in a call with her before I have to rush out in an hour. I'll call you when I land on Friday."

"Okay. Are there any cute doctors there? Any invite you to his room for a nightcap? Isn't that how it works on the medical dramas on television?" Candace joke.

"This isn't a television show. I keep telling you that. Stop watching those shows thinking that's what my life is like."

"That didn't answer my question."

"And it won't. Bye Sis!"

"Bye!"

As soon as the call ended, her phone rang again and

this time it was Zoe calling from her father's house.

"Zoe! I've been waiting an eternity to hear about your first day. I miss you so much. Tell me everything! Before you start, you're at your dad's house?" she asked.

"Yes. He picked me up from Gammy's house this morning when G-Pop was about to get in the car to take me to camp. He also picked me up when I was finished. I'm going to spend the night over here. He went to get us pizza for dinner."

"Okay, I'm happy to hear that."

"You fussed at him, didn't you?" Zoe asked.

Donna huffed.

"I did because he needed it. Sometimes adults need a little push to get back on track."

"Okay, well, my first day was fun and I have a new best friend. Her name is Brooklyn. We had a fun day."

Donna smiled bright even though Zoe couldn't see it.

"Tell me about it and tell me all about this new best friend named Brooklyn."

Donna settled in on the bed and let Zoe do all the talking. If this was the next best thing to being there, she wanted to give their talk her full attention.

6

"Dad, I had the best first day of camp. I mean, it was the best day ever!" Brooklyn yelled the minute she climbed into the backseat of the car.

Clayton relaxed after spending the day concerned that he would pick her up and she would tell him that she never wanted to go back again. They were barely in the car when she poured out all of her excitement over her first day.

"So, I don't have to try and find you a new camp?" he joked.

"No dad. Don't you dare. I had a lot of fun and I already have some new friends. One girl I really like, her name is Zoe and she likes the camp too. She's younger than me. She's nine. My class is for nine, ten and eleven-year-old kids like me. I think she's going to be my best friend. Plus, she had really good snacks, dad. You need to get me some cool snacks."

"Snacks? I pay for them to give you breakfast, lunch and an afternoon snack. I need to get you more snacks?"

Clayton laughed when Brooklyn looked at him wide-mouthed.

"Just some. I'll tell you the kind I want you to get. Snacks are big business at camps. When will I get a cell phone?"

"No cell phone. I told you that. You don't need one. Did kids have cell phones in your class?" he asked.

"No, not in my class. The older kids did. I know you told me no cell phone. You said I could keep asking."

He shook his head. His daughter was a challenge. He had to be on his toes to converse with her at eleven. He knew he was in for some real battles as she got older.

"Yes, you can ask as much as you want. No phone until you're a teenager and you have two more years."

"And I can get an iPhone?" she asked.

"Yes, you can get an iPhone. Now, back to the camp. What did you do today?" he asked as they drove through traffic.

"Oh, I have a paper for you about career day coming up. I forgot when. I want to be a doctor like you. Can I wear your shirt from Johns Hopkins? We're supposed to wear or bring something about what we want to be when we grow up. I told Ms. Shelia, my group leader, that I want to be a doctor and she said that was a great career. Guess what? My new best friend, Zoe wants to be a doctor too. She said her mom is a doctor. Isn't that funny? Me and my new best friend are going to be doctors. Can I wear one of your shirts?" she asked again.

"My shirts will be really big on you."

"Dad, we can tie it at my waste with a rubber band and make it fit. Please, can I?" she pleaded.

"Okay, okay. We'll make it work. Maybe aunt Selena can make it fit for you. We'll call her and see what she can do."

"Yeah!" Brooklyn cheered from the back seat. "I also signed up for swimming. I have a paper you have to sign. I told them I could swim, but you have to tell them. They don't believe me when I say it, I guess because I'm a kid. I like the reading group. The camp has a library with some good books. I already have a lot of them at home. I don't have arts and crafts until Wednesday and Friday. That's a bummer. Can we go to the store today so that I can get some stuff to make some bracelets? I want to make one for my new friend so that we can have matching bracelets. She's going to make something too."

"We can't go today, but we can go another day this week."

"Okay. Zoe likes to make stuff like I do; bracelets and necklaces and stuff. We're going to sit together in our classes. We ate lunch together today."

"Oh? What did you eat for lunch?" he asked.

"We had chicken strips with apple sauce. Also, carrots as snacks which I love. Do we have carrots at home? I want some carrots."

"Yes, we have carrots."

"Yum. Oh, I also had apple juice, orange slices and for a snack before you picked me up, we had peach yogurt, your favorite. I love my camp, dad. I can't wait for tomorrow. Can I eat breakfast at camp? They have French toast sticks for tomorrow."

"Yes. I was planning to drop you off for before-care for the rest of the week because I need to get to the hospital early. Aunt Selena is going to pick you up some to help me out. I still want to hear about every single day when we get home. I'm glad you like it and that you made new friends."

"I like the kids. Guess what? Me and Zoe like the same video games. She likes to go bowling and skating like me. Maybe you can ask her mom if we can go bowling or skating for a playdate. That would be fun, right?"

"Are you trying to ask me if you can hang out with Zoe for bowling or skating? I take it you and Zoe have already talked about this. Sounds like you want me to be the messenger with her mom. What about her dad?" he asked.

"I saw her dad this morning. You were sitting by the door during the program so you didn't see him in front with her aunt. She said her mother was out of town. She lives with her mom. Her dad has a different wife and babies. Can we ask if Zoe can go bowling or something?" she asked.

"I'll think about it. You have swim class tonight and

I will sign your paper to let them know you have been swimming since you were a baby."

"Thanks, Dad. Thanks for my camp. I really love it. Are you sure I can't have a cell phone yet?" she slipped in.

Clayton loved their back and forth about her getting a phone. At least once a day she asks and once a day, he tells her no. He wouldn't tell her that he was planning on getting her a phone for her twelfth birthday. He wasn't sure he could endure the daily asks for two more years.

"I'm sure."

When she snickered behind him, he knew she knew what she was doing. Oh, how he loved her. He'd made some good and bad decisions in his life, but one thing was for sure and that was, nothing would ever make him regret the love of his life in the back seat.

"Okay, I'll check with you again tomorrow," she said.

"Same time, same channel!" he cheered.

This time he did laugh out loud. His Brookie was the best!

7

"Welcome to Club Tremble!"

Clayton glanced over at the overzealous hostess who waved him through the throngs of people hoping to get inside of the newest, hottest club in Dallas. He chuckled at the wink and slight glide of her tongue across her lips as she eyed him from head to toe. Ignoring her, he followed her inside.

The grand opening was by invitation only, but that didn't stop hundreds of people from showing up with hope of getting in. He couldn't believe the blocks and blocks of people who stood in line waiting. Once he walked up to the large golden double doors at the end of a path paved with a long purple velvet carpet runner and purple and gold ropes, he knew he was about to be in for something special. Two steps inside of the club, the hostess turned him over to a waitress who took his drink order and pointed him in the direction of the VIP section where he was told to go to meet other guests of the owner.

As he walked, Clayton checked out the décor to his right with tables for seating with both high and low tables. There were tables meant for standing only, two large dance floors on the first level and an area where the live band was playing. He noticed two large bars packed with patrons and to his left was more seating, mostly comprised of booths with every seat having a perfect view of the band platform.

Reaching the wo steps that led to the VIP section, his eyes found Sebastian first who was nestled to the side between two giggling, gorgeous women. He gave him a nod and walked around greeting other friends as he took in the five-star treatment Will provided for them. Besides Sebastian, he saw Reggie, Patrick, Colin and Brent. Colin and Brent were friends he'd been introduced to through Will and who were now a part of their group when they hung out.

"This is crazy! As I walked over here, I couldn't see any of you through the glass. Now that I'm here, I can see everyone in the club," Clayton admired as he walked up to Sebastian.

"Yeah. I asked Shaba about that, and yes, he said it was okay for me to call him that and only me," Sebastian boasted. "He said the glass is one-way to give those in this section privacy, especially for celebrities. When they're here, he wants them to know that this is a place where they can have a good time, enjoy dinner, great music and company and not be worried about being seen. Not every celebrity wants the celebrity attention and for those who don't, he provides this. There are two other very open VIP areas on the other side."

"Yeah, I'm liking this, not that I'm a celebrity or anything," Clayton admitted.

"Really? I can't call it because I saw you when you first walked in and I do believe the eyes of every woman in this place were on you as you made your way here. Do you really not notice the attention you garner from every woman you pass by? Man, to be in your shoes sometimes!" Sebastian hollered.

"It's the walk," Patrick added.

Clayton and Sebastian turned when Patrick walked up to them and patted them on the back.

"Don't you start!" Clayton yelled over the music.

"Yeah, he's got that Denzel, Barack Obama type of pimp walk that the women love and swoon over."

"Hey, it's not a pimp walk; it's a walk of confidence and power," Clayton suggested. "You know my saying, *I am and I know it.*"

Clayton didn't see his life's mantra as ego, but as confirmation that his parents raised him to have confidence in himself if he ever expects others to have it.

"Oh? Can you teach it to us so that we can live a life where we can choose any woman we want and none of them will tell us no?" Sebastian asked and doubled over with laughter.

"Ah, I wish I could," Clayton beamed.

"What? Is it some kind of secret thing that if you showed us, you'd have to kill us?" Sebastian asked.

"Nah, nothing like that. It can't be taught, but maybe on someone else, it can be learned. Sebastian, you are a lost cause. Women are on to your game and a new walk won't help you!"

"Yeah, whatever. Being in VIP is already helping me. Did you see the two women hanging all over me when you walked up? It's been like that since I got here."

"And you?" Clayton asked Patrick.

"Man, y'all not getting me into trouble with my woman. My wife doesn't play when it comes to women. Trust me, I know better. Marcelle works with sharp objects every day as a surgeon. That's not the kind of woman you play around with. Besides, she's all the woman I will ever need. Reggie, I know you understand with the two of us being the only two in our crew who are married."

"Y'all met Selena. No more words need to be said. When she's yelling at the kids, I jump to attention too," Reggie kidded.

Clayton laughed knowing that no one played with Selena when it came to her kids and her man.

"I thought she was coming tonight since I was able to get a sitter for Brooklyn and didn't need to drop her at your house. Is she here?" Clayton asked looking around to see if he overlooked Selena somehow.

"She couldn't make it tonight. With the kids at her sister's house for the weekend, she decided to have a night to herself."

"Did you hook her up?" Clayton inquired.

He knew that Reggie loved the ground his wife walked on. Whenever he headed out and she didn't accompany him, he would lay out the red carpet for her at home.

"Of course. I grabbed a bottle of her favorite wine, I picked up food from her favorite Italian restaurant and I made sure her favorite music was programmed to play in the bathroom. A part of her nights to herself always involves a long, hot bath. She was all set. I even bought her some new stuff for when I get home," he declared.

"Marcelle joining us tonight?" Reggie asked Patrick, whose wife was a fellow surgeon.

"No. After a long week at the hospital, she also planned for a night at home to herself. I'm planning on joining her shortly for some quality time. I didn't want to miss coming out to support Will tonight. With this crowd, he wouldn't have missed me."

"Yeah, it's pretty amazing. I passed a table who were eating and I saw a steak that looked like it was screaming for me to order it," Clayton said.

"Man, you have no idea. There are several tables for us on the other side of the wall to your left with tons of appetizers from shrimp cooked four different ways, wings in so many flavors I lost count and something I've never had, but will be trying, deep fried lobster tails. There is food galore and that's just for starters. You can order anything you want from the menu. They have your favorite, porterhouse, which may be what you saw. I figured you'd want that," Sebastian offered.

When a waitress walked by with a tray of menus, Clayton grabbed one and checked out the choices. The first waitress handed him his beer and continued through the VIP section.

"Will Kincaid has officially put his name on the map! This menu has everything from soul food, to seafood to Mexican food. The drink menu alone is two pages long, two columns per page," Clayton admired flipping it back and forth to take it all in.

"He should be back in a few minutes. He's been checking back and forth to see if you had arrived. He wants to give us a private tour. If you look up, you'll see another glass enclosed area like this one. That's his office. He can see the entire club from there. He said it's the thing in clubs and restaurants these days. Speaking of our esteemed host, here he comes," Sebastian pointed to where Will was walking toward them, fighting his way through the crowd of people who were congratulating him on the major turnout.

"Yo!" Will hollered.

"You outdid yourself with this place," Clayton acknowledged.

"A life-long dream. I'm glad you made it," Will said.

"Yeah. I wouldn't have missed this for anything," Clayton said.

"How's little miss Brooklyn doing?" Will asked.

"She's great. Her favorite sitter is with her at the

house. I spoke to her before I got here and she said to tell her uncle Will congratulations on your new spot."

"I miss her. You'll have to bring her by to see the place. It's a family-based establishment until eight in the evening. We even have a large kid's menu. Wait until she sees that I created a menu item called the *Brooklyn*," Will boasted.

Clayton was shocked. He knew Brooklyn had one day teased Will about naming a sandwich after her.

"What? You actually did that? I thought she was kidding with you," Clayton said.

"She may have been, but I wasn't when I told her I would. I know she loves sloppy joe sandwiches and also grilled cheese sandwiches. I combined them together to make the Brooklyn, grilled sloppy joe and cheese on Texas Toast. Don't tell her. I want to surprise her," Will said.

"Man, thanks for that. She is going to be stoked. I won't say a word. I'll bring her by Sunday for lunch and you can spring it on her."

"Cool, that works. Say, let's make our way to my office. I want you to see the view from up there," Will pointed.

Clayton followed him along with the other guys. Instead of going through the crowd, they exited the VIP section through the back in a private hallway that was flanked by two of the largest security guards he'd ever seen.

After walking through a long hallway, they entered

an elevator, also flanked by security on both sides. Once they reached the floor above, they walked another long hallway which curved around as if they were circling the building. As they did so, Clayton checked out all of the signed celebrity photos that lined both sides of the wall.

"Man, you know everybody!" Sebastian said as they entered Will's office where the door automatically closed behind them.

"I've met a lot of them in my life, especially during my stint as a boxer. If you look out over to your left, the opposite side from where you were, there is another VIP room and you'll see some of the hottest artists and actors who couldn't wait to get in here tonight. They are also all over the club tonight. I have a few surprise performances tonight as well. This is an epic night for me. Thanks to Dr. Clayton Myers, I'm here and able to fulfill my dream."

The surgery, Clayton thought. Years ago, he performed surgery on Will who had been severely injured in a car accident. It was one that should have left him paralyzed. Coming through that surgery was a life changer for Will who had been living a wild and crazy lifestyle as a high-profile celebrity. Since then, they had become the best of friends.

"I hear that was some night. I wasn't on call the night they brought you in," Patrick noted.

"Yeah, I was in pretty bad shape, my own fault," Will admitted. "Life looks a lot better on the other side of that day. It's a reminder of how fragile life can be, especially when you live a life on the edge like I had been doing.

"I remember that night. Clayton wouldn't let anyone else touch your case," Sebastian said.

Clayton walked over to the glass and looked out over the club.

"When they told me who they were flying in from Las Vegas to Baylor, I didn't know how I was picked out of hundreds of qualified doctors around the country, including in Vegas. I got word that your team of doctors requested me specifically to operate on you due to the severity of the spinal injuries you suffered. Everyone who saw the accident between you and that truck assumed you were a loss cause. Not only did they not expect you to ever walk again, some even thought that you wouldn't make it off of my table. I knew the job. It wasn't just to keep you alive, but to make sure you walked again. Every second was critical," Clayton said.

"You are the bravest man I know because I heard my doctors saying how bad it was and that even surgery could potentially make it worse. One small mistake and I would be flat on my back for the rest of my life. Yet, you still took it on and here we are – four years later and not only am I walking, but I'm running. I'm thankful for every single day. I will never take my life for granted again. I've been an advocate against drag racing ever since. I'm just glad the only person I injured that day was me and not someone else. I wouldn't have been able to live with that."

"You never moved back to Vegas?" Sebastian asked.

"Not even for a day. I love Las Vegas, but that's not a place for me. There were always too many temptations for me to act a fool. After my surgery and an entire year spent in rehabilitation, I felt like Texas was my home. Clayton turned out to be one of my best friends and the rest is history! Now, here we are. One of the first people I wanted to celebrate with is not any of my celebrity friends, but with the friend who saved my life in more ways than one."

Clayton started to turn his attention in Will's direction until a vision in white caught his eye. He found himself unable to look away. It wasn't just the body-hugging dress trimmed in silver around the neckline, the matching white and silver stilettos on her feet or even the incredibly shapely, killer body that danced with confidence in the middle of the large dance floor. There were plenty of women moving to the Reggae beat, but this one woman, he already knew was masterfully created. He zeroed in on her as if this moment of recognition was meant to be. His body, mind and spirt knew her. His heart recognized her. His eyes locked in on her and even if he wanted to, he couldn't tear his gaze way. When she flung her long hair over her shoulder, threw her head back and laughed as if she didn't have a care in the world, he felt like a moth to a flame. She was here. Clayton couldn't believe it but the woman who'd been on his mind lately was occupying the same space.

"Donna," he said softly.

"What?" Will asked.

"He said Donna. I don't think you know that story, Will. Clay, what about Donna?" Sebastian asked.

"It's Donna. She's here. Look. She's here on the dance floor."

Clayton heard shuffling behind him as Sebastian and Patrick flanked him at the window where he pointed to her.

"Damn!" Patrick shouted.

Soon, Will, Colin, Brent and Reggie joined them where all eyes landed on Donna and all of her exquisiteness.

"Who is she?" Will asked. "There's a story I don't know?" he added.

"Yeah, there is. She's the one that Clayton let get away."

"Clay, man – what were you thinking? What the hell are her flaws that you walked about from all of that? She is gorgeous. Is the sexy woman next to her with her? They look alike," Will asked.

"Yeah, that's her sister, Candace."

"Their parents got it going on popping out beautiful women like that. You let her slip away?" Will added.

Clayton knew he would have to explain himself since only he, Patrick and Sebastian knew the whole story of what happened.

"I didn't actually let her slip away. We were engaged when I was back at Hopkins. We were both doctors at the same hospital and I messed up; I mean, really messed up," he explained.

"Brookie?" Will asked.

"Yeah. Don't get me wrong; I love my daughter more than life itself. Messing around with her mother cost me my relationship with Donna. I screwed up big time, literally and figuratively."

"That's the Donna you told me and Selena about?" Reggie asked.

"The very one. Damn, look how good she looks," Clayton mumbled to himself, but loud enough that the guys heard him.

"Was she always that fine?" Will asked.

"Yes!" Sebastian responded before Clayton could.

Clayton growled at Sebastian who threw his hands up in surrender.

"Whoa, I would say we should all stop ogling her. Clayton is pretty touchy about Donna," Sebastian said.

Clayton didn't care about any of them. He couldn't take his eyes from Donna who was dancing pretty close to some guy who appeared as taken with Donna as he should be. In his arms was a woman that any man would be grateful to have. She was smiling and locking eyes with the man. Clayton was jealous of what appeared to be a familiarity between the two of them. He was angry and feeling possessive when he didn't have a right to be.

"She lives here now?" Will interjected.

"Yeah, she moved here recently. She's a pediatric surgeon."

"Beauty and brains? Is she still single?" Will asked.

Clayton turned his burning vision to Will and grimaced.

"Whatever you're thinking, don't even go there," Clayton warned.

"I told y'all he was touchy about her," Sebastian said.

"I wasn't saying it for my benefit, but for his. If she's single like he is, perhaps he can reconnect. She's here tonight, he's here tonight; I say go for it," Will suggested.

"She's with someone," Clayton said, finally turning away from the window and finding a seat on the long, black leather seat where he didn't have to let jealousy take over as he uncomfortably spied on her. "That ship sailed a long time ago. I'm sure she's moved on. Did you see her with that guy? They weren't just dancing; they know each other. They're possibly dating or married or something, I don't know. Let's talk about something other than my failed loved life," Clayton added.

When Patrick changed the subject back to the club and began tossing out one question after another to Will, Clayton was thankful for friends like him who had his back. He faked paying attention to them while his mind was on the temptation to walk back over to the window. Seeing Donna in photos on the hospital website and in her minimal social media presence, he wasn't prepared for actually seeing her in person. He had survived without her all these years because they were in two different places in their lives. Now that she was here in the same city, he wasn't sure he could escape the old feelings that have once again surfaced. Tonight, they were more potent than ever.

He couldn't believe that seeing her again had him feeling nostalgic enough that he held a tinge of hope that she was close enough to him now and perhaps, her heart had softened toward him. He could only hope. Hearing his name called, he rejoined the conversation in the room. In the back of his mind, a small voice was telling him that he would have a chance to find out for himself. He didn't know when. He smiled to himself knowing that he was a patient man.

8

Donna slid onto the high chair at the high, square table that Candace was able to secure for them. Joining them was Lance, the man her sister thought would be a great match for her. She had to admit, she was skeptical of her sister's knack for setting her up on a date, but in Lance, she did find a connection once they hit the dance floor. They could both dance.

Lance had arrived shortly after they had. When he walked up to her and Candace at the entrance with another man in tow, she was presently surprised at her sister's pick for her. Lance was handsome, not as tall as she was used to when it came to men, but when he smiled her way, his happiness in seeing her appeased her. In her high heels, he was the exact same height as she was. While Lance introduced himself to her and shook her hand, she gasped at her sister when the man who walked over to them behind Lance walked over to Candace, leaned down and kissed her, not on the cheek but on the lips. It was cute and sweet, but she had questions for her sister.

They had been in the new club for about thirty minutes when Lance had asked her to dance. She had enjoyed learning about him, though a few minutes into the conversation, he started talking about the woman he'd been living with who left him for another man almost a year ago and he was still stewing over it. She could see that he was still hurt from it. She let him talk, thinking he would get it off of his chest, but that didn't happen until he finally asked her to dance.

Candace and her date, Jonah, were already on the dance floor when she and Lance joined them. She had to admit, that Lance had some great moves which paired very well with his attire for the evening, black dress pants and a long-sleeve black shirt, opened around the neck to show a large tattoo that traveled from his chest, up and around his neck. Lance also sported a large diamond earring in one ear, his only jewelry for the evening. She did notice, even before they ventured inside the club, that he was wearing *Versace Eros* cologne for men; one of her favorites. She loved a good smelling man. She actually thought that there may be some potential to get to know Lance beyond the night.

At the table with the four of them seated, Jonah offered to get a round of drinks for everyone. When he stood to leave and was joined by Lance, Donna finally had a chance to chat with Candace before they arrived.

"Good choice, right?" Candace asked before she could toss out her own questions. Together their eyes watched the men until they disappeared into the crowd between them and the main bar.

"He's nice," Donna said.

"Nice? That's all you've got? He's more than nice."

"I just met him."

"I know, I know. I just thought he would be a good fit for you when I met him at Jonah's launch of his new construction company. They're business partners, working together on major projects for the city."

"This is how you let me know you're seeing Jonah? I know you said you were seeing someone, but I didn't know that he was who you were talking about. I've watched him kiss you a few times. When did you become okay with public displays of affection?"

"Girl! He's so delicious, right? You like him?"

"Candace, if you like him, then yes, I like him for you. As long as you're happy, it's all good."

"True, but it's not anything serious. He's not who I was talking about when I told you there was someone I wanted to talk to you about. I'm just sowing some of my own wild oats. I'm having fun, for now."

"When did you become this wayward? There's another guy? Really?"

"It's someone familiar," Candace offered.

Donna thought before she tossed out another question and then she knew.

"Are you and hubs thinking of rekindling? It's funny that you've mentioned him several times this week. He seems to be at your house even though Grace was away at camp."

When Candace shrugged her shoulders, Donna knew she was on the right path.

"I don't know, maybe. I don't want to talk about that right now. There is some smoke and maybe a little fire again between me and Terry. I just want to have some fun tonight. We can talk about that another time. Jonah is fun. What about you? Do you think you'd actually go out with Lance on a date? I can tell he's really into you. He can barely take his eyes off of you. Fact is, I don't think there's a man here tonight who can take his eyes off of you. Why didn't you tell me that you had this kind of body under all those scrubs and business suits? I mean, I've seen you, but hooked up like this, it's been a long time since I've seen this look," Candace kidded.

"You know I love to work out. It's my stress reliever."

"Well, Lance could be an additional stress reliever for you. Have you seen his walk?"

"Why is your mind always on a walk and how a man uses his legs? You do know there's more to men than what they can do between the sheets!"

"Spoken like a woman not getting any!"

"I'm over casual dating and casual sex. I want more."

"Maybe you can get that more that you want from Lance; you never know unless you're open to it."

"Sis, I know you mean well, but can I tell you

something?"

"Anything."

"Since the moment we sat down to talk while you and Jonah hit the dance floor, Lance has done nothing but talk about his ex-girlfriend and how devastated he was that she broke up with him."

"What's wrong with that? Maybe it's still fresh."

"It was a year ago. That's not fresh at all – that's obsessive."

"Wow. Really?"

Donna nodded her head.

"That left a sour taste in my mouth. It's odd for a man to go there with a woman he may be interested in, but okay. I'm not saying I wouldn't go out with him again. In the conversation, he pretty much said he wasn't ready for anything serious yet, but he was open to testing the water. Testing the water? I am not to be tested on. Look, I appreciate you trying to look out for me, but I can get my own dates. I really can find my own man."

"From the looks of every man looking your way, I believe that. I just thought it would be cute to double date with Jonah and Lance."

"We don't have to date men who are friends in order to do that. I'm still getting settled in. When I start dating someone and we can double date, you'll be my first call."

"Okay, I get that. I'm sorry if you're not having a good time with Lance."

"I am having a nice time with him and with you. I'm glad you talked me into coming. I haven't danced that much in a long time. We're going to keep enjoying our night. We'll try out some of this good food on the menu, drink some good wine and have the time of our lives. Our girls are safe and secure and we have the whole night ahead of us. Besides, Lance can dance his ass off! Did you see his moves? You know how much I have always loved dancing. He's been the perfect dance partner. You did good and I appreciate it. I'll let you know how things go. Like you said, I won't know until I dive in, right?"

"That's what I'm talking about!"

"White wine for the ladies," Jonah said as he and Lance rejoined them.

"Thank you," Donna said as Lance handed her a glass.

"You know, you are a very beautiful woman. I know you hear that all the time. I wanted to say it again just in case you forgot I mentioned it already," Lance said taking his seat next to her.

Donna turned her full attention to him. She hadn't done a lot of dating after splitting with Benny. Now that she was in a place that she planned to stay for good, loving she was near family again, perhaps Lance could be what she needed in her life. She was more than open to finding out.

"Thank you again. I appreciate each and every compliment," she acknowledged.

"That's good because I feel like I need to throw my hat in the ring to possibly get you to go out on a date with me before all of the eyes from the men in the place step up and act. Do you notice the attention you garner? I can see why because you are stunningly beautiful."

Before she could respond, Lance took her hand and kissed the back of it, keeping his eyes on hers.

Donna wiped his slate clean and decided to open herself up to the possibility. She was absolutely ready and maybe, just maybe, Lance could be it. She leaned in close just as Lance spoke again and commented that she was much more beautiful than his ex. He then proceeded to tell her all of the things that he was lucky to escape when she broke up with him. Her expectations tanked. She smiled anyway.

9

Clayton sat on the front row amongst the other parents of the campers as they waited for the career day program to begin. He was happy to have been able to move some meetings around at work so that he didn't miss Brooklyn's presentation on how she wants to one day be a doctor just like him. As interested as she was in medicine, she reminded him of how he was at her age. Everything interested him about medicine and healing people. Brooklyn showed the same desire and interest. Anytime he got the chance to help her foster a path to medicine, that's what he did.

The night before, she made him sit still in the family room while she went over her presentation with him, including pictures and all. The assignment for Monday morning was to create a board using pictures from magazine to explain what she wanted to be when she grew up. He started helping her with it last week, but other than collecting magazines from friends for her to use, she wanted to do everything herself.

When they arrived with her dressed in one of his Johns Hopkins Medical School shirts, which had come down to her knees before Selena helped alter it, he watched her happily wave at her friends who were excited to see her in a doctor shirt. It was now the cutest shirt, tied at her waist and worn over a pair of denim shorts.

"Hello."

Clayton turned around and faced a woman with long, blond hair and the bluest eyes he'd ever seen. He smiled her way and extended his hand.

"Hello. I'm Clayton Myers."

"Yes, I know. Your daughter is the lovely little girl with that long, thick black hair. She's beautiful – as pretty as you are handsome. Does her mother braid her hair so pretty like that all the time? I just love it. I'm Jessica. My son is in Brooklyn's class. I've seen you a few times when you dropped her off. I assume that's your wife I've seen pick her up sometimes?"

Clayton laughed to himself. Camp hasn't been going on long enough for someone to already know his drop-off and pickup routine. When she took the seat next to him and leaned over, her breast were close to falling out of her sheer white tank top which showed a bright red bra-like top underneath. When she flipped her blond hair over her shoulder and tilted her head to the side to try and connect with him, he shifted a little in his seat to put a little extra space between them.

"No, that's not my wife. I'm not married. She's a family friend who helps me out with Brooklyn when my schedule gets busy."

"Oh? What do you do, or am I prying?" she asked, shy-like.

"I'm a doctor and as you can imagine, my schedule can be pretty hectic. Thankfully, I have a pretty good village when it comes to Brooklyn."

When Jessica tried to hide her ring finger, he was quicker than she was. He noticed it before she placed her hand behind her. She was too late and she knew it.

"I guess you saw my ring. I'm married, but my husband and I have an, how shall I say, open marriage. If you need another person in your village to help with Brooklyn, I'm more than will to help. I'm a stay-at-home mother and I have a whole lot of time on my hands. My husband is a pilot and he's gone a lot. Two of our kids are here at this camp and another is spending the next couple of weeks at a young engineer's camp at a local university. That gives me a lot of free time to myself," she offered.

Clayton had no doubt, but he wasn't biting. He couldn't believe how forward she was being and right here in the middle of the camp.

"Well, you know, I think the village is pretty full right now. Besides, I make my daughter a priority. I tend to move things around as much as I can to give her my time and attention."

"I understand that. You must find that you need

your own time away to do non-kid things. You never know; an additional friend in your village could have lots of benefits," she said, trying to reel him in.

Clayton chuckled, playfully and looked down at Jessica's hand where she placed it on his arm. Knowing that she was being inappropriate, he moved her hand just as Brooklyn walked over to them.

"Daddy?" she asked.

"Yes, sweet pea."

He turned giving Brooklyn his full attention.

"Zoe isn't here yet. Are you going to stay for the whole program?" she asked.

"Yes, I am. I'm not going anywhere until it's all over. I wouldn't miss your big day."

"You must be Brooklyn. My, aren't you a real beauty," Jessica said.

When Brooklyn looked from him to Jessica who was still sitting too close for his comfort, he gave her an eye that said she shouldn't be rude. The smirk on Brooklyn's face was one he recognized. It looked a lot like one her mother used to give people; the one that showed tolerance but not interest. He nodded her way and she knew what to do because he'd taught her respect.

"Um, yes, I'm Brooklyn."

"I'm Tyler's mother, Miss Jessica."

"I know Tyler. He likes to eat dirt," Brooklyn offered.

Clayton held himself in tact knowing he would talk

to her later about her comment. He wasn't sure how Jessica would respond until she did.

"Yes, he does that at home too. It's a terrible thing, but kids do strange things that they eventually grow out of. Maybe you could be friends," she said.

"I'm friends with everybody. He's okay. Daddy, can we go outside and look for Zoe and her mother? We're doing our presentations together since we're both going to be doctors."

He turned to Jessica, using this moment as a chance to move away from her. Women are a lot bolder these day in going after men. He was used to attention from women. He didn't find it appalling that women were more outgoing when it came to a man they find attractive. He wasn't interested in Jessica, mainly because of the wedding ring on her finger. She had nothing coming from him.

"Jessica, it was nice meeting you."

When she stood and nodded his way before walking away, he exhaled knowing Brooklyn had just saved him from an uncomfortable conversation.

"Why was she being nice to us? She's usually mean and screaming at Tyler and his sister. She even cursed at him one time when he wasn't moving fast enough."

"She was just being nice. All the parents were waiting and she came over to say hello, that's all."

"Okay. Can we go look for Zoe?"

"I don't think we need to do that. If she's coming, I'm sure she'll be here soon. The program doesn't start for another fifteen minutes."

"Maybe her mother had doctor stuff to do. Her dad may bring her. You can ask her mother if we can have a play date though. Please, please can you ask her?"

Clayton patted the seat next to him for her to sit in.

"I told you I would ask her and I will. I have to meet her first or Zoe's father. If she brings Zoe today then I will ask her today. I have Friday after work or Saturday during the day free. If you want to go skating or bowling or something, I am free."

"What if Michelle comes to visit? I won't be able to hang out with Zoe."

Clayton's skin crawled every time Brooklyn called her mother by her first name. He didn't correct her often because it would only cause confusion when Michelle was around. She didn't like being called mommy, momma, mother or anything else that resembled those words. Now that she was older, he just went with it to keep the peace and to not have Brooklyn try to figure out what to call Michelle and when.

"She's not coming this weekend. I already told her that I was off the entire weekend and that I wanted to spend time with you doing whatever you wanted to do. I've been so busy at the hospital lately that I thought we could use some much-needed time. If you want to do a playdate with Zoe and her mother or father are free to bring her to meet up with us, I'm all for it."

Brooklyn hugged him tight and he pulled her close.

"I'll go wait for Zoe in the other room. You know, if

we do the playdate with her mom, you can talk doctor stuff. Remember I told you she was a doctor like you and even went to Johns Hopkins like you. We could both have a playdate. Is that what it's called for parents on a playdate with their children?" she asked.

"I'm not sure, but doctors always have lots to talk about. It'll be fun. Let me know when Zoe gets here and you can introduce me to her mother or her father, okay?"

"Okay, daddy. I'll be right back. She may be in the other room already."

Brooklyn ran off. Before he could get comfortable in his seat, he turned to cross one leg over the other in the opposite direction and when he did, on the other side of him, a woman took the seat right next to him that Jessica had vacated. He shook his head knowing he was having some morning.

"Hello. My name is Claudia. I hear you're a doctor. Was that your cute daughter? I have a daughter around her age. Maybe we can set them up on a playdate soon. I'm single and I understand you are too?" she asked.

Clayton looked beyond her and watched as Jessica appeared to snarl at them from a distance. Word travels fast, is all he thought as he listened to Claudia toss out even more questions before he could answer. He couldn't wait to tell Sebastian about all of this. If he did, he was sure that at Brooklyn's next camp program, Sebastian will be front and center looking for the women to flank him. He would eat it up.

"He leaned back in his chair and listened because he was unable to get a word in. He wasn't going to be rude but he hoped the program would be starting soon.

10

"Mommy, what time is it?" Zoe asked from the back seat of the car for the tenth time. Donna knew she was running late, but this morning, it couldn't be helped. She had to take be on an early morning call about the process for getting a patient on the kidney transplant list, if that's what was needed for five-year-old Jackiel Olmos, whom everyone called Jack. She was asked to take the meeting in person, but she persisted on a conference call knowing she didn't want to disappoint Zoe.

"It's five minutes past the time you asked me five minutes ago," she answered, smiling at Zoe through the rearview mirror where she sat holding her presentation for the morning program tight in her hands.

"I don't want to be late."

"I promise not to make you late. We're just about there."

Donna was happy when she finally pulled into the parking lot, driving slowly around to try and find a parking space. She checked the time and technically, they weren't late yet. She was glad because Zoe had been looking forward to this day for a week. They spent hours working on her display board and finding the right old Johns Hopkins t-shirt for her to wear. That searched helped her unpack even more clothes.

"Did I tell you that Brooklyn's dad does surgery like you?"

"Oh, really? I don't remember if you did tell me. I've been so busy lately. I'm sorry if I forgot."

"Yes. She made up a song about her dad being a doctor and it's funny," Zoe laughed to herself.

"A song? She's very talented. She must love her dad if she made a song for him."

"She does. She loves him to the moon and back, she says all the time. The song is called, *My Daddy Doctor Clayton*. Do you want me to sing it?"

Donna slammed on her breaks, causing her and Zoe to jerk forward.

"Sorry about that," she said.

"Why did you do that?" Zoe asked, looking at her stunned.

Donna heard a name and wasn't sure she was processing what she heard. It couldn't be. There was no way this was possible.

Finding an empty spot, she pulled into it, turned off the car and turned around to face Zoe.

"I didn't mean to. I wanted to get this space. You said something about a song. Is Brooklyn's dad's name

Clayton?"

"Yes. She calls him dad, but she told me that was his name. Did I tell you she calls her mother by her first name and not mommy like I call you? Do you want to hear the song? I could make up a song for you, if you want me to."

"Sure, baby. I would love a song."

"Mommy, you look strange. Are you sick? Can you wait to get sick after my program?"

"No, I'm not sick. I might be a little hungry."

"Oh goodie. They have snacks inside. Can I get out now?" Zoe asked.

"In a minute. Do you know Brooklyn's last name?"

Donna could feel her pulse quicken as her mouth went dry. Maybe her worlds were not colliding in the craziest, unbelievable way. Can't be, she thought.

"Um – oh yeah, it's Myers. I don't know how it's spelled."

If there was ever a time for the ground to open up and swallow her whole, this would be it. There was no way that there would be two Dr. Clayton Myers', both surgeons and both living and working in Dallas who was also at Johns Hopkins.

"That's okay, I know how it's spelled."

She knew more than his last name and the spelling of it. She knew the man. Donna needed a moment. Was Clayton here? Was she about to see him? What kind of game was life playing with her? She thought back to how old Zoe told her Brooklyn was and with a quick calculation in her head, there was no doubt that Brooklyn was Clayton's child with Michelle.

"Mommy, I need to get out. Can I go now? I want to see if Brooklyn is here."

Donna couldn't move. She thought she was ready for the day, but not for this. Did Clayton know about her? Did he know that Brooklyn's friend Zoe was her daughter? She was about to find out. She couldn't wait any longer and disappoint Zoe. They had to get out of the car. She inhaled and found the strength to come face to face with Clayton. She thought she would have more time for an encounter with him. She was definitely over the hurt, but being completely honest with herself, she wasn't over her desire and love for him. He was still the one and only man she'd ever really loved with everything in her. He had hurt her, but after twelve years of missing him, he still held a place in her heart. She was about to see what that meant.

**

Clayton caught a break from a third mother who found her way to the seat next to him. Thankfully, one of the fathers of another child walk over to him, recognizing him as a fellow doctor. They were in the middle of a conversation about the best football team in the NFL when Brooklyn came running up to him with another little girl followed close behind.

"Daddy! This is Zoe, my best friend."

Clayton looked over and smiled at Zoe, giving her his hand to shake.

"Well, hello Zoe. It's a pleasure to meet Brooklyn's best friend. She talks about you all the time."

"Hello," Zoe answered.

"Can we have a playdate? Her mom is here for you to ask her. We only have a minute, daddy. We have to get ready to start," Brooklyn explained hurriedly.

Clayton stood, looked up and froze in place. He looked from Zoe to the woman who walked up behind her and for a second, he forgot how to breathe; *Donna*. She was Zoe's mother? Brooklyn's best friend was Donna's daughter? All kinds of out of this world thoughts ran through his head. Their daughters were best friends and they didn't know it? At least he didn't know.

"Clayton."

The melodious sound of his name formed and spoken from her perfect lips awakened a desire in him that he hadn't experienced in a lot of years; not since her. He's seen and experienced his share of beautiful women, but not made his heart skip beats like it was doing right now; all because Donna showed up like a breath of fresh air. Not only did his eyes recognize her, but his body screamed with untamed familiarity. He felt a sudden chill in the air, followed by intense heat radiating from within.

He had no words as his eyes took in the fact that she was standing in front of him. He looked her over, not caring who could be watching them. She was beautiful; more so than ever, even more than the

Friday before, a few days ago, when he stalked her all night from a distance at the club. He lied to his friends when he said he loved the view from Will's office so much that he preferred to spend the evening there. He couldn't muster up the correct words that his truth was he hadn't prepared himself for actually seeing Donna. If he went back to the VIP section, he ran that risk. Will obliged and had lots of food and drinks brought up to the office. To his surprise, even Sebastian controlled his desire to hit the dance floor. Clayton knew his friend had his back. If Donna saw him, she would know that Clayton would be somewhere close by.

See Donna sucked the air out of his lungs as he perused everything about her. Her hair was down around her shoulder. She was wearing a pair of jeans that hugged her just right. She always had the perfect body for jeans, leaving tongues hanging out as she walked by. She stood on top of high heels that gave her legs a sexy, statuesque look with toes peeking out at him painted in a soft, pale green. She had on a matching green top, tied at her waist with the buttons opened and revealing a white tank top underneath. Her makeup was soft and alluring and he couldn't stop staring at her. By now, he was inching into a stalker-like phase. If it were not for Brooklyn tugging on his shirt, he would have never looked away. He was too afraid she wasn't actually there.

"Daddy, we have to go. Playdate?" Brooklyn asked again, smiling up at him with all of her teeth showing.

He looked down at her.

"Let's talk about it after the program. You and Zoe need to get going. I see your teacher waving for you."

When they ran off, he was left standing in front of Donna, stilled by the surprise of seeing her. The coincidence was unimaginable, but in a good way; at least he hoped so. Other than saying his name, she hadn't said anything else. Perhaps she was holding in her anger because the girls had been standing there.

"Hi, Donna."

"Surprised?" she asked.

"You have no idea," he replied.

"Me too. I found out a few minutes ago in my car that you are Brooklyn's father. Zoe talks about her nonstop. Just a few minutes ago, she mentioned a song Brooklyn made up about her father the doctor. When she told me the name of it and I heard your name, I couldn't logically put things together until I actually walked in and here you are."

"Even when Brooklyn told me that Zoe's mother went to Johns Hopkins, there was no way I would have put that all together. I found out just now, when you walked up. This is crazy, crazy, right?" he asked.

"The craziest thing that has ever happened to me. What are the odds? Seriously, what are the odds of our girls meeting here at camp and becoming best friends? This is beyond crazy," she acknowledged.

"Yeah. I would say this is some kind of *Twilight Zone* kind of thing."

When Donna laughed, Clayton let out the breath he'd been holding in. Perhaps, this wasn't going to be a bad meet and greet; sort of. Remembering what happened the last time they faced each other, he wasn't sure what to expect.

"Ladies and gentleman, please take your seats. We will be starting in ten minutes. This is your last call for drinks and snacks. We ask that there be no walking about during the children's presentations. If you already know that you need to leave early, please take a seat in the back of the classroom as not to disrupt anyone."

When neither of them moved, Clayton didn't know what to say or do. He had so many things running through his mind that he wanted to express, but he knew now wasn't the time. Was Donna really here standing in front of him? Would he be wrong to embrace her and open up about how much he's missed her? He still had so much to apologize for. Was she still hating on him for what he did? What should he say next?

He snapped out of it when Donna's soft hand touched his bare arm. The hairs all over his body stood at attention.

"Clayton, I see the wheels turning. Rest assured, I'm okay and so are you. What happened with us was a long time ago. I've moved on from that. I'm not angry anymore. In fact, there is no way I can be angry at this point. Our daughters are best friends. Imagine that," she said.

Clayton let his shoulders relax, feeling the tension leave his body. He didn't want things to be awkward between them. Most of all, he didn't want anything to mess up his daughter's happiness. He and Donna are now forced to figure out how to deal because like it or not, Zoe and Brooklyn are in control of the next steps.

"I'm glad to hear that. Why don't we sit. Brooklyn had me save an extra spot for Zoe's parent and that's you, of course."

When Donna moved to take her seat, he waited and sat back down as others around them began sitting as well. Just as they had, he saw Jessica and Claudia walk toward him, eyeing the seat that Donna had just sat in. Both walked away grimacing at her causing him to shake his head in disbelief.

"I see you still have that affect," Donna noted.

"What?"

"On women. Those two women just gave me the death stare."

"Well, you know how women can be. This seat is reserved. I would have to deal with my daughter if I didn't save it."

Donna's bright, beautiful eyes connected with his. Just like the very first day that they met many years ago, not at the hospital but at a small takeout spot opposite the hospital, her eyes, filled with hope and promise radiated through him. He didn't fall in love that day, but he refused to leave the quaint place with the best cheesesteak subs in East Baltimore, before he got her number. Like then, her eyes pulled him in and wouldn't let him go.

"They want a playdate. What are we going to do about that? They don't know about our history, at least Zoe doesn't," she said.

"Brooklyn doesn't either. We can't tell them no to a playdate. What would be the reason?" he asked.

"I wouldn't think of it. Zoe making friends is important to me. We just moved here recently, right at the end of the school year. Zoe had to leave all of her friends in New York and I was afraid she wouldn't have enough time to make friends before school let out. She only had a few weeks before summer break started. They've bonded and we can't take that away from them."

"I wouldn't want that," Clayton responded. "Brooklyn has a nice size group of friends, but none of her friends are here at this camp. I wasn't sure how she would handle making all new friends this summer. She connected right away with Zoe."

"So, a playdate?" Donna asked.

"Yes, definitely. Brooklyn mentioned roller skating or bowling. I would say bowling."

"We need to sync our schedules. Not to be in your business, but Zoe mentioned you and Brooklyn live alone. You're not married? Should you confer with her mother before making a date, you know, because of our past?"

"Michelle and I are divorced. We weren't married long and I have full custody of Brooklyn. She doesn't live in Texas."

"I'm sorry things didn't work out."

"What about you? Brooklyn mentioned Zoe lives with just you?"

"True. I'm divorced as well. I share custody with her father who has remarried and has two small children. He lives nearby, but I pretty much plan out Zoe's schedule."

"Same for me. Sounds like we can plan a date around our two schedules. I'm sure when the program is over, we'll get the playdate question again. I'm pretty swamped during the week, as I'm sure you are too. What about the weekend? Friday, Saturday or Sunday can work. I was already scheduled to be off."

Donna pulled out her phone. He watched her scroll through her calendar.

"The weekend looks good for me, too. What about bowling on Saturday afternoon. I don't know a lot about the area, but perhaps you do?" she asked.

"That I do. I take Brooklyn bowling twice a month, depending on my schedule. There is a place not far from the camp that we can go to. She went to a friend's birthday party there recently and the place is very family friendly; not a lot of rowdy older kids. Maybe take them for burgers and fries after, if that works for you?"

"Perfect. Zoe loves a good burger and milkshake."

Clayton laughed out loud and then covered his mouth after his outburst. He leaned close to Donna.

"So does Brooklyn. I think it's going to be interesting finding out all of the things our girls have in common."

"I agree. This is so strange. No eggshells, though, okay? I don't want anything to be awkward. The past is the past."

Clayton shook his head agreeing. He would have said more but just then, all of the kids filed out of the adjourning room holding their projects in their hands. They were about to begin.

Turning to focus on Brooklyn, he would never speak it out loud, but he whispered a silent thank you. He couldn't have asked for a better start to his day than this. He never could have planned anything this good. He couldn't wait to see what was next. For now, he winked at Brooklyn when she smiled, beaming at him with pride.

11

After the program ended, Donna shared a few more words with Clayton before Brooklyn and Zoe walked over. Before they could ask, she told them that she and Clayton had already talked about the playdate and it was scheduled for the weekend. As the girls jumped for joy and ran off, all of the parents walked around and greeted each other. She was hoping to get a few more words in with Clayton, but the room seemed to get more crowded. Knowing she needed to get to the hospital, since camp was actually just starting, Donna found her way through the crowd and out to the parking lot.

For the first time since seeing Clayton, she was able to exhale and shake off all of the nervousness she felt sitting so close to him. They didn't get the chance to talk during but they clapped and he whistled when Zoe and Brooklyn completed were finished with their presentations, complete with toy stethoscopes. She remembered picking up Zoe's earlier in the week and it was clear, Clayton had done the same. Other than the color difference, the objects were the same.

She was still taking in that he had married Michelle and was now divorced from her. There was no doubt in her mind that when she heard Michelle was pregnant, Clayton would do what he considered the right thing and marry her. She was sorry it didn't last, but if he was now happier, then it was a good thing.

She never cared for Michelle and Brooklyn was the innocent one in all of that. She watched Brooklyn during the program and she was a very happy little girl. It was clear how much she loved her dad. Even while presenting, she would find a second to secretly wave to him, glance his way and smile. When she looked over at Clayton, she saw a father whose daughter was his whole world. She always knew he would make a great father. She just didn't expect that it wouldn't be with her. That was now water under the bridge. Like she told him, they had both moved on.

When her phone vibrated, she nearly jumped out of her skin. Reaching for it, she answered before Candace had a chance to hang up.

"She did wonderfully," Donna said the minute she answered. She already knew why her sister was calling.

"Like I knew she would. She's brilliant like her aunt! I knew she would kill it," Candace exclaimed.

"Yeah, whatever. She gets her brilliance from her mother."

"Yeah, but she gets her beauty from her aunt! Are

you still there?"

"I'm just getting in the car about to head to work. Where are you?"

"At the salon. I have a full day today with clients back-to-back. I wanted to slip in for Zoe's presentation but I didn't think I could get back in time for my first client. I forgot to try and reschedule her. Did you at least record it for me?"

"No, because the camp recorded it and all the families will get a copy. I'll make sure you get to see it. I did take a few pictures of her and Brooklyn. They presented together; two doctors in the making."

Donna knew that was her in to tell Candace her other news. She was dying to tell her since the minute she knew.

"Did they? That's wonderful. You finally got a chance to meet Brooklyn. It's she the cutest little girl. I met her once when I stopped by to check in on Zoe when I was in town. She couldn't wait for me to meet her new best friend. I guess the move here wasn't as bad as you thought it would be, especially at the end of the school year."

"Candace, you will never guess in a million years who was at the camp today!" Donna blurted out. She couldn't hold the words in any longer. "Not only that, you will never in a lifetime guess who Brooklyn's father is."

Donna nibbled on her index finger, still feeling giggly about today's revelation. When her leg started tapping up into the steering wheel, she smiled at how nervous she still was even though Clayton was nowhere around.

"You know I've hated guessing games since we were kids. I could guess tons of names and would probably never get it so just tell me."

"Okay, are you ready? I'm serious. You can say you're ready but you won't be. Are you sitting down?"

"Girl! If you don't stop with this. No, I'm not sitting. I'm standing up doing hair. The suspense is killing me. Let me hear it!" Candace yelled.

"Clayton Myers."

"Clayton? What about Clayton?"

"He was at the camp today."

When Candace didn't say anything else, Donna was tempted to let her words sink in, but she was taking too long.

"For what?"

"Okay, get this; he's Brooklyn's father. Zoe's best friend is Clayton Myers' daughter. They are one in the same!"

Donna bounced around in her seat unable to contain her excitement. She had been tame when she encountered Clayton, but she had to let the jubilance out. She was finally able to speak the words to someone and it felt good.

"Wait, what did you say? Did you just say that Clayton is Brooklyn's dad? Are you serious or playing games with me? I have not had coffee yet. I'm not up for games this early in the morning."

"You heard me. *The* Brooklyn that Zoe is friends with is Clayton's daughter."

"What!" Candace shouted.

Donna heard a clash and knew that Candace had dropped her cell phone.

"Shoot. You made me drop my phone. It's a good thing the screen didn't break or you would be paying for it. You can't spring something on me like that in a casual kind of way. That's *big* news. How in the hell did that happen? Is this the daughter he had with...?"

"Yes, it is. Now that I saw her and him in the same room, she looks exactly like him. She's a beautiful version of how handsome he is."

"Well, what did you say to him? Anything?"

"Yeah. I said hello."

"That's it? You couldn't think of anything else to say?"

"I mean, we talked about the girls having a playdate. I could tell he didn't know how to take my presence. I told him the past is the past and our girls are friends. He agreed that they are the priority. He did save me a seat right next to him. I was sitting so close that I could smell his cologne. Check this out, he wears, *Sauvage* by Dior. You know what that does to me when a man smells that delicious. He smelled and looked like everything I always knew he was. I don't think he's even aged. He was so sexy."

"Enough to make you want to jump him right

there?" Candance laughed.

"Only you would say that," Donna flippantly responded.

"Stop playing with me. How in the world is this possible? Do you know how big Texas is? How big Dallas is? How could it be that you both happened to put your daughters in the same summer camp and they end up as instant friends. You live a perfect life. I swear you do. I mean, lady luck lives all up in your life. What are the chances that after we were recently talking about him that your daughters would bring you together in the same room?"

"I know. We talked about how crazy it was that this strange story is our lives. No matter how you look at it, yes, it happened."

"He looked really good, huh? Scrumptious as always?"

"Better. I'm serious. If there was ever a man who has aged to perfection, it's Clayton Myers."

"What's his story? Married? Girlfriend? What?"

"He's divorced. He married Michelle, but he said it didn't last long. He has full custody of Brooklyn. Michelle doesn't live here. That's all I know. I didn't ask about a girlfriend or anything."

"Did you tell him you were divorced?"

"I did, but Zoe had already told Brooklyn, though at the time, there were no names exchanged."

"So, you found out when you got there."

"I found out in the car when I pulled up. I was

talking to Zoe and she mentioned some song that Brooklyn made up about her father and in the title was his name. I asked about her last name and when she said Myers, I damn near peed on myself. Seriously, I was that shocked. I almost second-guessed going inside. I had to for Zoe, but I was scared that he might actually be here. I didn't know what to say or do if he was actually here. Of course, he was and it wasn't bad at all. Oddly enough, we were comfortable with each other."

"What's next? Did he ask you out? Did you ask him out?"

"No. We agreed to a playdate for the girls over the weekend. We're taking them bowling. He knows a place."

"Did you schedule a playdate for you, too? It's been how long for you since you've been invaded? You know what I mean."

Donna gasped.

"Really?" she asked Candace.

"Don't act like you just met me. I'm looking out for you. I'm trying to get you a workout. There was a time when that man had you sprung on that good loving."

"True. See where that got me?"

"Yes, I do. It's got you in a position where your life has come full circle back to some unfinished business. You're single. He's single. Make something happen. That man once loved you. He messed up, but who hasn't. Men have done worse to women. Even you said that's in the past. Your girls didn't just out of the blue meet each other. It's destiny baby! Call and ask him out."

Donna started to respond and instead, her mouth hung wide open. She forgot to get Clayton's number.

"Shoot. I didn't get his number to confirm the outing. I'm sure I'll run into him one day this week when he drops off or picks up Brooklyn. I'm in town all week, so Benny won't have to do it."

"Right. Or you could call him at work since you know where that is."

"You are so right. I can do that too."

"Wrong! I was joking. You are so easy. Get your behind out of that car, go back inside and get his number. Is he still there?"

"I left before him. He was caught up in a myriad of women who were stepping on each other to get his attention. You should have seen two of them. I thought they were going to claw my eyes out. All I did was sit in the seat next to him."

"That man is a chick magnet and you know that. I bet he didn't care anything about that once he laid his eyes on you. You are not someone to cast to the side. You can hold your own going up against any woman. You just choose not to. Again, how long has it been?"

"Whew. Way too long. Seeing him I was reminded of how long it's been since I've been with a man. What is wrong with me?"

"Nothing came out of getting to know Lance?"

"No. I sat through him pining over his ex-girlfriend and I didn't think I could sit through that again on a date. He did call me yesterday. When he asked what I was doing, I mentioned I was looking over some research files and cooking dinner. He went into a downward spiral about all the good meals his ex would cook on Sundays. I can't with him. He needs to shake it off."

"Let's forget about him and focus on Clayton. Are you over what happened enough to go out with him? Maybe entertain something more?"

"Yes."

"Well, damn. I thought you would take a few minutes to think about it."

Donna laughed at herself.

"You know what? I thought so too, but that would be a waste of both of our time. I saw him and the only history I thought about was when we were together and not what happened with that woman. Candace, I was supposed to be happy with that man. I hooked up with Benny when I was vulnerable and he was looking to settle down. I leaped without looking because I was hurt and Benny gave me attention. That marriage was doomed from the start. Don't say I told you so. I know you called it and told me not to do it."

"I wouldn't do that."

"I know. I just hate that I went through that with Benny when I never should have. On the flipside, if I had not, I wouldn't have my Zoe and I can't imagine that. I messed up by tossing Clayton into Michelle's arms so fast. Men have babies all the time. Look at Gabrielle Union and Dwyane Wade? You know how much I love that couple. She never looked back after finding out he made a child even if it was when they were on sort of a break. I think their hearts were still connected just like Clayton and mine was. He tried to get me back. He tried really hard to get me to give him a second chance. I wouldn't hear of it."

"Don't do this to yourself. You can't go back. What you can do is go forward. You and Clayton are in Dallas, you're both single and you reconnected by way of your daughters. How much more of a perfect storm do you need to know that this was meant to be? Look, I need to focus on my client. Think about it. Get that man's number and if you see even a small sign that he may be interested in you, I expect you to take that and run with it. You are being given a second chance. Don't you think you deserve it?"

Donna had a lot to think about. She didn't know if she was bold enough to walk back into the building just to ask for Clayton's number. She needed to think.

"Get back to work and call me tonight. I need to get to work too. Love you, sis," Donna said.

"Love you too."

When Candace hung up, Donna sat in her car and decided to think about things later. She needed to get to work. Putting her car in drive, she pulled off. She knew she would run into Clayton again soon. She sure hoped so.

**

Clayton had reached his car and was about to open the door when he stopped. He knew he would see her when they took their girls bowling, but that wouldn't be the time for them to have the conversation he really wanted to have with her. She wasn't married. She didn't appear hostile toward him as if she still hated him for what he did. He wasn't known for being a man who shied away from a challenge, even if the end result wasn't in his favor. Now wasn't the time to become a person who didn't go for and accept every challenge.

Searching the parking lot, he spotted Donna at the other end pulling out of a parking spot, in a BMW coupe with the roof down. He imagined her flying down the expressway with her hair blowing in the wind, looking like a model. Seeing that she had to come toward him to get out, he walked into the roadway a waved her down.

"Hi, again" he said. "I saw you leave and thought you would be gone by now."

"I should have been. I called my sister and that was a lengthy conversation. I was just thinking about you."

Clayton perked up.

"Really?"

"Yes. I realized we didn't exchange phone numbers for the playdate planning."

"True. I was thinking the same thing. If one of us has to cancel, you know the life of a doctor, we need to be able to reach each other."

Clayton took out his phone and typed in her number as she read it out to him. When she was done, he sent her a quick text so that she would have his number. The moment she smiled in a shy-like fashion, he knew why. He'd sent her a text that said, *'thank you, beautiful'*.

"Thank you."

"You're welcome. You are, you know. You are still so incredibly beautiful as you've always been. I hope that isn't overwhelming to say. I don't want to embarrass you. You can tell me to kick rocks, if you want to. I'd understand," he admitted.

"I wouldn't do that. I appreciate the compliment. You haven't aged a day yourself."

"Thank you. Are you headed to work?" he asked.

"I am. I have a little boy that is being added to the kidney transplant list. It was inevitable. I thought I would have more time for the possibility of other options. I need to meet with his parents. Are you working today?"

"I am. Being chief of surgery, I don't do as many surgeries as I used to, but I try to schedule at least one a day for myself. I don't want to hold you up. I'm glad you were still in the parking lot. I'll call you to finalize plans for the girls. Are you okay with that?" he asked.

Clayton was hesitant to say that he was also anxious to talk to her again. Now that he had, he wanted to continue doing so and not just in conversation about their kids.

"That works great for me. Call me anytime," she offered.

"Anytime?" he asked and waited.

He knew his eyes were locked on hers. He wasn't even sure he was blinking; too afraid a blink would take away from the time of having his eyes on her. He was a goner for her again. He didn't think this was the time to ask her out on a date even though that's exactly what he wanted to do. The words were on the tip of his tongue, but he held back. Hopefully, there would be another chance.

"Yes, anytime."

Clayton moved back from her car and returned her wave as she drove away. Walking back to his car, he knew he was going to take advantage of the opportunity that Brooklyn and Zoe provided. The day would come and he would be ready. He only hoped Donna would be just as ready.

12

Clayton exited the operating room, exhausted but gratified that his third unexpected surgery of the day was complete. With a day that started with introducing new interns to the residents they would shadow for the next few months, he hadn't planned on ending it so late with an emergency surgery for an abdominal aortic aneurysm. What should have been an uncomplicated three or four hour planned surgery after the patient complained of back and belly pain, turned into an emergency once the patient's abdomen was opened for the surgery and there was a discovery of a more complicated medical issue going on.

The resident who started the surgery called for assistance and with other surgeons tied up on working on patients from a major multiple car crash, he stepped in. He still had a staff meeting with the team at the private medical practice that he and Sebastian ran together. This was a lot for a Thursday, but it was also the life of a surgeon and he loved every minute of it.

Heading toward the lockers to change out of his dirty scrubs, he turned in the direction of Sebastian calling as he walked out of the operating theater, the glass enclosed room that overlooks the operating room. It's where surgeries could be observed.

"Where have you been all week?" Sebastian asked.

"Busier than usual. Have you not seen the new batch of interns who started today? It was postponed from Monday because of the hospital emergency and then here we are today with another emergency. Things have been crazy. What's up with you?" Clayton asked.

"I've been helping cover the emergency room all week. Today was complete madness. I was checking on you to see if you're still doing the staff meeting at the practice tonight. If not, maybe grab a beer before you head home?"

"Staff meeting, yes – beer, no. I want to get the meeting out of the way and introduce the three new doctors we're adding to the private practice. It's growing fast. We now officially have two floors in the office park building. There is new equipment coming and new office furniture for the additional doctor's offices. Did you handle the hiring of two new front desk executive assistants? Me and you need to sit and discuss plans for any other new hires."

"That's exactly why I offered us grabbing beers tonight. I did a couple of interviews this week and I like them all. I have my top choices picked and I want to run them by you. I emailed you what you needed to look at. When I didn't hear back, I knew it was because you were busy. It's also time we hire a second human resources director and take all this kind of work out of our hands. We know we're expanding, yet we're slow with making the changes we need to make."

"I hear you. Can we do that next week? Perhaps, Monday?"

Clayton didn't want to tie his weekend up with anything work related. He had that playdate scheduled for Brooklyn and if he played his cards right, he might get Donna to agree to having dinner with him before the end of the weekend. It was a shot in the dark. Things don't always go the way you want them to, but he was counting on fate continuing to operate in his favor.

"Monday? There are a lot of days between now and Monday," Sebastian noted as they entered the locker room. "What about the weekend? Unless you're working."

Clayton had yet to tell Sebastian about how and where he ran into Donna the week before. While he had a minute to himself, the perfect time was now.

"I have weekend plans. I made everyone aware that this weekend is mine and I'm not willing to share it. I secured all the coverage needed here at the hospital and at the practice."

"Big plans?"

Clayton smiled.

"Something like that."

"What gives? I know that look. You're up to something. Better yet, what's her name?" Sebastian asked.

After a brief hesitation, Clayton spoke the name he hadn't said to anyone else.

"Donna."

"Donna? Donna who? Do I know her?"

"Donna, man. Did you not hear me?"

When the name registered, he watched Sebastian go through an exhaustive display of shock and awe.

"Stop playing. Donna, Donna? Where have I been and why am I just finding out about this? I expect to hear everything. You're not leaving here until I do."

In less than five minutes, Clayton ran down everything to him from finding out that Brooklyn and Zoe were best friends and how Donna turned out to be Zoe's mother. After telling him about the playdate for the girls on Saturday, he explained his plan for asking Donna out on a date.

"That's what's been up with me."

"I'm going to need you to write this down for me. I plan to sell this story to some romance writer. No one would believe that your two daughters found their way to each other and became best friends. Your daughter and Donna's daughter. That's so outlandish that it's believable. Seeing her that night at the club wasn't just a fluke. It's a prelude to reconnecting with her. You ready for that? Is she?"

"I don't know if she is, but I am. This happened on Monday and since then, all I've done is think about her. I'm so ready that I've looked for her each morning when I dropped off Brooklyn. I've been dropping her off earlier than usual at before care so that I could get to the hospital early. You know Selena picks her up for me. I was all out of sorts sitting in my car waiting for her to pull up just to get another look at her. She's gorgeous man."

"When you talked with her, was she still upset with you? Any ill-will at all? What about when she saw Brooklyn? She had to reminisce about how Brooklyn got here."

"We talked about that and she confidently shared that she had let all that go a long time ago. Then, I saw her in the parking lot after leaving the program and I swear we had a moment. It was strange considering how long it's been since we last saw each other. Being around her and talking to her, I felt like I was back at Hopkins when things were good between us. Man, she smiled at me and made my day. I've been itching to just call her to say hello, just to hear her voice."

"Bruh, how are you sprung like this? I've seen you date women over the past few years and I've never heard you talk about any of them like this. In fact, I've known you since you and Donna dated back in the day and I have never heard you talk about *ANY* woman like this. Real love, bruh. Real love."

Clayton sat down on the bench in front of a locker, trying to remember the combination, but his mind wouldn't rest from thinking about Donna.

"I have beat myself up for a long time over what happened. Even now, I still can't believe I was so stupid."

"Stop that. We were all wild. We thought we ran that hospital. It was easy to get caught up in the ego trip we were all on. You're not the only person to blame. Didn't you tell me Michelle came clean about what she did to you?"

Clayton nodded. He hadn't thought about that night when Michelle moved out and told him the truth about what really happened. He didn't hate her for what she did, though he was angrier than he's ever been with her. If they weren't already breaking up, he would have ended things. Like Sebastian said, he wasn't the only person to blame, but his lack of control had him caught up. He'd missed many years that could have been spent with Donna.

"Yeah, but the damage had been done. I married Michelle because she was pregnant and a month after that, Brooklyn was born. There was no turning back at that point."

"Look, you're an honorable man. You always have been. We're best friends because you balance out my bizarre personality; you keep me sane. You did what you felt was the best thing for you and your daughter. I respect that and hurt or not hurt back then, Donna probably understands that. She doesn't foster any hate now because she knew that once Michelle became pregnant, the baby would be your priority. You tried to mend things and Donna didn't want that. Fast forward to the here and now and it's possible that you could go back and not change things, but set your life with Donna back on track. What are you going to do? Look, I'm going to head out. I'll meet you at the practice for the meeting. Don't make this a long one. I don't have anything scheduled until around noon tomorrow, so I'm hanging out tonight to play pool. You're welcome to join, of course."

"Nah, I'm good. I'll keep the meeting short. I want to get home. Brooklyn is with the sitter. I haven't talked to her today because I've been so busy. I want to have a few minutes with her before she goes to bed, if I can."

After Sebastian gave him a thumbs up, Clayton removed his scrubs and headed into the shower room. He turned on the water full steam to wash off the remnants of a heavy surgical day. Stepping under the steady stream, he leaned his hands against the wall ahead of him, lowered his head and closed his eyes. In the quiet of the room with nothing other than the sound of the water cascading down around him, he couldn't help but think back to the conversation with Michelle that Sebastian referenced.

That last night together had been a volatile one with her. He'd finally learned the truth and it had cut him like a knife. Even now, remembering reminded him of what he'd lost. He was cocky and stupid. If he'd never gotten with her, she wouldn't have been in a position to get one up on him. She reminded him of that as she was packing to finally move out.

"Where are you going to go?" Clayton asked Michelle as he watched her quickly grab everything she could from her closet and dresser drawers, tossing things haphazardly in a suit case and other bags she'd brought in from the garage.

"Why do you care? Have you ever even cared? Do me a favor and not answer that. This whole marriage has been a lie. No time for truth now. I think I've had enough truth to last me a lifetime."

Clayton watched her fiery disposition from his vantage point from the seat at the foot of their bed; a bed they hadn't shared in months. He had moved into the guestroom when he was tired of living the fakeness that was their marriage. Neither of them wanted to be together. He didn't see a reason for them to continue.

"Did you want to keep living this farce of a marriage? Come on. We ran off and got married. We didn't have any family or friends with us. We used strangers as our witnesses. Hell, your family didn't even know you were getting married. We've been married for two years and I've never met anyone in your family."

"Yeah, well at least I knew better than to expose you to them. My family is full of a bunch of nuts. I wouldn't even call them my family. I never liked them

and they never liked me. I'm good with that. As for your family, they never liked me. You can now tell them they no longer have to fake smile at me. I know your mother despises me. She's always telling me how to hold my child, how to feed my child, how to wash clothes. She's the queen of the kitchen, thinking I wanted to hear about how she's kept her husband all these years because she could cook. I didn't care every time she opened her mouth to tell me about all the things I do wrong," Michelle spit out.

"You're entitled to your feelings, but don't disrespect my mother. She may not care for you, but she's never disrespected you. She has nothing to do with this. You're leaving because we didn't work out!" Clayton shouted and then caught himself. Brooklyn was sleeping in her room across the call from them. He didn't want to wake her. At her age, she'd heard enough of their fights. That was all they ever did.

"No, I'm leaving because you asked me for a divorce. You're filing tomorrow, right?" she asked.

"If you want to file, I'm fine with that. One of us needs to. It's been a year of this back and forth, non-stop fighting."

Michelle stopped, turned around and came to stand in front of him.

"Did you ever love me at all? Be honest with me about that. Did you ever love me? If anyone asked you, would you ever be able to say that sometime over

these past years that you were in love with me?" she asked.

"No," he admitted.

Clayton knew his response would hurt, but he was tired of lying. They both needed to find what was for them and it wasn't each other.

"You bastard!" she yelled.

"Michelle, you knew. You have known all along that I married you because you were pregnant. I'm not trying to hurt your feelings. You said be honest and I'm doing that. If you were honest, you would admit the same thing. You never loved me either. You wanted to be a doctor's wife. There was never any love between us. We had sex and it resulted in an unplanned pregnancy. We both know that no protection is one hundred percent and we never slept together without any. Things happen. What didn't happen was me falling in love with you or you with me. Why can't you be honest and say what this was all about?"

She didn't respond. He watched her storm back into the closet to grab more clothes. She went back and forth four or five more times before she finally stopped moving and turned toward him again. This time, she hit him with a sinister laugh unlike any he'd heard from her before.

"You know what? Let me give you some truth. That's what you want right? The marriage is over. I'm leaving and there's no turning back. I know where you

stand and I'm going to be fine. You want some real truth? Here it is. My pregnancy was not an unplanned pregnancy. See, what you don't know is that you were so busy trying to bed all kinds of women behind Donna's back that you let your guard down. I swapped out your condoms with ones that I had punched a hole in. I wanted to get pregnant. I was tired of you and Donna prancing around the hospital like the happy couple ready to get married. Two doctors planning out their perfect life together. You were far from perfect and she was oblivious to anything around her when it came to you. I poked a hole in an entire box of condoms at a time when I was most fertile. That's how I got pregnant. It wasn't unplanned; I planned it. You men are so feeble-minded thinking with the wrong head all the time. You see a sweet ass of a willing woman and the blood rushes in the wrong direction when it comes to common sense. You fell for the okey-doke, sweetheart. How is that sitting with you! I was the cause of you losing your precious Donna, miss perfect. I hated her. She had you and I wanted you. It was that simple."

Clayton sat emotionless, though that wasn't the reaction he wanted to have. He was too stunned by her revelation. She'd tricked him? She'd set him up to get pregnant knowing he was engaged to marry Donna? Yes, he was caught up in the attention he garnered, but he never thought she would be that devious. She'd kept that from him all this time.

"Michelle, tell me you're lying. Tell me you did not do that!" he yelled at the top of his lungs.

"Yeah, well, I did. How you like me now?" she asked. When she laughed in his face, he knew they were on dangerous ground and she needed to leave sooner rather than later. He thought about Donna and what his mistake had done to her. Now he knew that Michelle had set him up on purpose and he was furious. He was tired of engaging her. The marriage was over and he couldn't go back and fix the past.

He stood to walk out and stopped moving when Michelle flinched when he towered over her.

"You don't need to be afraid of me. I've never given you a reason to be. I'm not that kind of man and you know it. Trust me – a lesser man would probably be on his way to jail right now. I'm not that man. I do want you to finish packing and go ahead and leave. We need a lot of distance. What you did was deplorable, but it's done and it can't be changed. I'm going downstairs to my office. I don't think there is anything else that needs to be said or done besides you finishing up here. We'll see each other in court."

"I need to get some of Brooklyn's things and her playpen. I'll need something for her to sleep in until I can come get her furniture."

Clayton had been moving toward the bedroom door when he stopped after hearing the line that Michelle had just crossed if she thought she was taking *his daughter anywhere. He turned and walked back over to her.*

"You're not taking our daughter anywhere. You don't even know where you're going. If you want to leave, you go ahead and do that, but you're not taking Brooklyn anywhere until I know where and that she'll be safe. You're flighty and Brooklyn can't be a casualty. I offered to let you stay here in the house and I will continue to pay the bills. You don't work. What are you going to do?"

"I have friends."

"Who? You piss off everyone you know. Look, you can make whatever decisions you want for you, but until you have a stable place to live, this is Brooklyn's home. Feel free to take me up on my offer of staying in the house and I'll get a place nearby. Brooklyn will not be snatched from her house and forced to live a nomad life with you. Have you forgotten that you have a habit of disappearing for days, weeks at a time? Was Brooklyn a priority any of those times? Look, I would never keep you from her, but you're not in a position to do what she needs if you leave here. The choice is yours. You're saying that you want to take Brooklyn with you and you'll be fine with that? Think of her, right now, and not yourself. If you tell me that you believe Brooklyn would be better off leaving this house with you and you mean it, then I will hate it, but I'll let you take her. Don't take her to hurt me, though. This marriage was crap from the start and you know it.

Brooklyn is innocent in all of this. Do you really want to have her every day, all day? If you say yes, then I'll help you pack some stuff for her."

He waited. He may not love Michelle, but he knew her, sometimes better than she knew herself. One thing he was sure of, though he hated to admit it, was that she never wanted to be a mother; she wanted to be married to a doctor. She used the scheme she thought would get her there. Brooklyn was two years old and Michelle still had not bonded with her. He had to think of his daughter at this moment. She is who mattered in all of this.

"Can I come see her whenever I want?" she asked after calming down.

He had calmed as well, though his blood was at the boiling point.

"Absolutely. I would never, ever keep you from her. I only want what's best for her."

"What about after the divorce?" she asked.

Michelle would never openly admit it, but she was looking forward to having her freedom back and not just from him, but from her responsibility as a mother. He wouldn't hold that against her. His concern was their daughter.

"I'm willing to share custody equally."

"That would mean living with me half the time and then living with you half the time?" she asked.

"Exactly."

Michelle started fidgeting; shifting from one foot to the other, biting her fingernails. She was vulnerable because she knew her truth and so did he. She needed to say it. He couldn't do this next step for her. She had to speak it.

"If I give you full custody, will you let me see her and spend time with her? You're right that I don't know where I'm going or where I'll be. That's not a life for her. She's so little."

"Yes, she is. You will always be able to see her anytime you want. She's as much yours as she is mine."

When she turned back to packing, Clayton turned back to the door.

"You can have custody," she whispered.

"I'll let you finish."

"Clayton, wait."

He stopped but didn't turn around to face her. He was done talking, but he would let her say her peace.

"What is it?" he asked.

"I'm sorry for all of this. I know that everything that has happened is my fault. I also know that you're a good man. I wasn't thinking when I set all of this in motion. I wanted to get with the hottest doctor in the hospital and that was you. I wanted you to look at me like you looked at her, but you never did. You never looked at me with love; not that deep, unconditional love I know you had with her and I was jealous. I did want you, but I didn't want this life. I know you

offered for me to stay in the house with Brooklyn, but I feel caged here. I feel like I can't breathe. I don't think I'm meant to be a wife and mother."

"Why are you saying all of this now? There's been enough hurt already."

"You're the best parent for Brooklyn. I could never give her the attention she needs. I want to be free. To do what? I don't know. Don't hate me for not wanting this life."

"I don't hate you. You'll always know how to reach Brooklyn and see her anytime you want. Are we done?" he asked.

"Yes."

Clayton nodded and left the room. He could hear Michelle continuing to whisper that she was sorry. At this point, so was he.

Hearing noise out in the locker room, Clayton brought his mind back to the present and away from a memory that wasn't a good one. He and Michelle were able to patch things up enough to deal with issues around Brooklyn, but he never looked back on those few years together. He was now thinking about his future and if he could really put his path to love back together. It's along the lines of wondering if you could ever go home again. He hoped it was possible for him and Donna.

13

Candace tried her best to keep her eyes on Donna as she raced around her bedroom chasing one drop-dead gorgeous dress after another.

"You are acting as if you've never been out on a date before. This is Clayton. Remember him? You've dated him before. Why are you so nervous?"

Donna paused and turned to Candace, glaring at her with eyes filled with annoyance.

"I know who it is and that's why I'm nervous. Maybe I shouldn't have agreed to this date. Maybe Clayton and I should have left things with our daughters being friends. Why, oh why did I say yes?" she blared out.

Grabbing a form-fitting little black dress and holding it up in front of her as she glanced into the floor to ceiling wall mirror, she thought that this was probably the dress for the night, or maybe not.

"I like that one. Go with that one and save me from another hour of putting dresses back in your closet only to watch you pull them out again for a third and fourth look. You will look good in everything you put on with that killer body of yours. Besides, if you take much more time looking for a dress, Clayton will be here. We've been at this for over an hour and I'm sure Brooklyn and Grace are getting hungry. I think I can hear their little stomachs growling from over here."

Donna sucked her teeth and smiled.

"I'm being extra, huh? I know. It's just that this is Clayton. Can you believe that? I can't even believe I'm saying it out loud."

"Tell me again how this date came about?" Candace asked.

"I think I prefer the powder blue one. I love how I look in blue and it's sexy. Wrap dresses always make me feel sexier than any other kind."

"You want to look sexy."

"I do, right? I mean, it's Clayton."

"You are doing the most. Tell me how the date came about. You only told me he asked you when you asked me if Zoe could spend the night with me and Grace."

"Oh, I didn't tell you? Let me try the blue dress on again and I'll tell you while I'm doing that."

Donna raced into her closet for the first dress she'd tried on at the start of the evening."

"I'm listening!" Candace yelled at her from where she lay on her back on the bed.

"Well, the girls were bowling and having a real

good time. I was having a good time too. Clayton and I ended up joining them and then the real fun began. I will say that, though he beat us all score wise, Zoe and Brooklyn both beat my score. I was outscored by two kids!"

"The story?"

"Oh, right. Anyway, after bowling, we went for burgers. The girls wanted their own table. They got a booth and Clayton and I shared one where we could keep our eyes on them."

"What did you talk about or did you just eat in silence?"

"Of course not. We talked about everything that doctors talk about. He wanted to know about my research project. You know how excited I get talking about that. He then talked about his private practice. I told him I had been thinking about doing some additional consulting and starting my own business. That got the conversation really going. He gave me a lot of good tips. I talked about this patient I have, a little boy who needs a kidney. That case has been troubling me. There is something I think the mother is not telling me. Anyway, we talked about the girls' schools. He asked about mom and dad. He told me how his parents were doing. He also mentioned a house he bought last year that's on the beach. He called it his getaway spot. He and Brooklyn go there when they want to relax from everyday life. It sounds amazing. He's done well for himself."

"So have you. Did you tell him about all the awards you've won?"

"I did. I asked about the coveted awards I know that he's won. We realized that we only knew about each other's accolades because we must have been keeping up with each other's careers. That cat was out of the bag."

"Sounds like you had a good time. Sounds like old times with the two of you, except the night didn't end in good, hot sex! Maybe tonight will. You sure could use it!"

"Stop it. Anyway, after we ate, he and Brooklyn walked us to our car. I admit, the playdate for the girls had gone really well. Now they want to go roller skating."

"Ugh – you are dragging this out."

"You're so impatient. You should work on that."

"Okay, we'll work on my faults another time. My stomach is growling. Hurry up already!" Candace yelled.

Donna walked out of the closet and stood in front of the large floor to ceiling mirror.

"Yes, I think it's going to be this one," she said, admiring herself.

"I agree. You look amazing in that. Blue is definitely your color. I love when you wear blue makeup. You look exotic."

"Thanks. This is it."

"More!"

"When I got home and Zoe was in taking her bath, he called me to thank me for letting the girls hang out. We talked about how we see that they can be best friends. They have a lot in common. When we were getting ready to hang up, neither of us said goodnight. We listened to each other breathe. I felt like he wanted to say something. At the same time, I really, really wanted him to ask me out. I felt like we both wanted to do that the whole night, but neither of us did."

"Were y'all making those googly eyes at each other across the table? I bet that was cute!" Candace joked.

"Being real, yeah, we did and yes, it was cute. After some very painful silence, he finally blurted it out and before he could get the last word out, I had already said yes. We both laughed out loud. He asked about dinner having dinner tonight and that was that. We ended the call and I went to bed with a huge smile on my face."

"Like now?"

Donna looked at her face in the mirror and she was indeed smiling. She couldn't help it. Knowing she was going out on a date with Clayton hand her tingling all over. There were places on her that no man had awaken in a long time. Clayton had always been different from the moment they first met.

"Yes, just like now. Am I overthinking this? Maybe it's nothing more than two old friends having dinner. I may be overselling this to myself."

Just like that, the excitement left her body and she wondered if she was making more out of the date than

Clayton was.

Realization set in and she plopped down on her bed next to Candace and exhaled loudly. What was she doing? Why was she doing it? She knew why. Clayton Myers was still the finest man she'd ever laid eyes on and the way he still looked at her made her heart skip a beat and her body, shamedly quivered at his piercing light brown eyes. The man still had it going on.

"Don't you dare start questioning your reason for saying yes to him asking you out. There is nothing wrong with the two of you stoking a fire again. Contrary to what you may be thinking right now, that man asked you out because he's interested in you. It's all perfect if you ask me. The planets are aligned, the stars are shining tonight and with the full moon that's planned for tonight, it's a perfect setting for animalistic howling!" Candace shouted and laughed.

Donna laughed along with her and then covered her own mouth as if she'd said something wrong.

"Not so loud. The girls will hear you. Did I tell you thank you for coming here to pick up Zoe tonight? I was going to bring her to you and then I got caught up in a last-minute meeting this morning that ran over."

"No worries. When I got here and told Zoe she was coming with us, she ran straight to her room with Grace in tow and they started packing her suit case. I saw Zoe pull out her sleeping bag too. I swear, I bought Grace those bunkbeds but every time she has a sleepover, she and her guest end up on the floor instead."

"I'm grateful for you. This isn't Benny's weekend and I don't feel like answering a bunch of questions from him either if I ask him if Zoe could spend the night."

"You know I would move heaven and earth for you and my niece. She can stay the rest of the weekend if you want. Just in case you and Clayton decide that you want to, you know do that deed since you're all backed up and stuff."

Donna reached to punch Candace on the arm but missed her as she rolled out of reach. Knowing Clayton would be here soon and she didn't want him to run into Zoe, she hopped up to finish getting dressed. She only needed to select a pair of heels and some jewelry and she'll be done.

"There will be nothing like that going on. I told you, it's just dinner."

"What if it's on the table? Supposed you have a chance to get with him tonight? Are you saying you would turn him down? Look, I know you've been out of the real dating game for a long time, but this is Clayton. Being with him intimately isn't something the two of you have to act all new about. You've done it with him. Many times, I might add. It's a new day and women are not shy about their wants and needs. If you want him, why not go for it? What happens is between you and him; well, and me because I want all the details. You've always been in love with Clayton. I think while you were married to Benny you were still in love with

Clayton. Feel free not to admit anything along that line. I love you and I don't want you to regret this chance like you regretted walking away before. This dinner is your olive branch. If you feel it, do it. You have a free night all to yourself. You don't have to work tomorrow and you don't have to worry about Zoe. I'm assuming it's the same for him. Take advantage of tonight. I know I sure as hell wouldn't pass up the chance to be wrapped up in the arms of the only man I've ever loved."

"Oh yeah? What about your ex-husband? You seem to be talking about him a lot lately. What's going on with that? You thinking about doing the deed with him? You told me recently that he was slipping through your house for visits even though Grace was away at camp."

"I already am, if you must know."

Donna almost tripped trying to slip her shoe on while standing. It wasn't the shoe's fault. It was hearing Candace's response.

"What? Y'all are getting it in? When? Why? Are you back together?"

"Yes, we are. When? All the time. We're doing it more than we did when we were married. That man can still get it. I'm throwing it at him every chance I get. The season will be starting soon, so he'll have less time, but I miss him. I miss being married to him."

"I thought he was seeing someone. Don't tell me y'all are creeping behind her back? You know better."

"I wouldn't do that. He's not seeing her anymore. We're thinking about giving things a try again. I'll let you know how that goes. Tonight is about you and what you're going to do. Don't forget, I was with you through that breakup. I flew from Texas to Maryland and stayed with you for a week while you cried. I know what it was like for you then. You need to grab onto whatever it is you want from Clayton and hold on; if given the chance, don't let go."

"You've always liked Clayton, haven't you?"

"I did and I still do, but you're my sister and I love you first. I could have throttled him back then. I also know that people make mistakes. You have always been that person who is hard on others. You don't allow much room for errors in judgement, at least you didn't used to. You changed after you had Zoe. You became more tolerant of people not being perfect. I'm not saying that to chastise or judge you and you know it. When you finally found your own footing in your career and you chose pediatrics, a dam broke loose within you and out poured a heart of gold and a compassion that you haven't always had. There is nothing wrong with that. You're a different person now. Think about that. Think of who you were back then and what you allowed in your space. Think about your expectations of those close to you then and now. You should be able to see the difference in what you accept and don't accept. You're different. Clayton is different. Perhaps you're both different enough that now is the time. You get what I'm saying?"

Donna understood completely. She remembered a different Donna back then and Candace was right; she didn't give people many chances to make-up for their wrongs. Things were her way or no way. That's not who she is now.

"I get it. I don't sound silly saying that I would jump at another chance with Clayton? I'm definitely not delusional about my desire to jump him, but to be involved with him again? I would take that in a heartbeat. I knew it the minute I saw him standing in that classroom looking like the perfect gift to have under my tree for Christmas."

"Hey, I say don't wait until Christmas to unwrap that tall, handsome, chocolaty wonder. Get yours and don't look back ever again. Your cell phone is vibrating on the bed."

Donna watched Candace pick it up.

"It's Clayton. He said he's on his way."

Donna looked over her shoulder when she heard Candace shuffling around on the wood floor.

"You're leaving?" she asked her.

"Yes. I'm hungry and I know those girls are ready to go. Besides, Clayton will be here and you don't want to explain to Zoe why he's here and there's no Brooklyn with him."

"Right. Okay, go ahead. I'll call you in the morning. I can either pick Zoe up or let me know if you want to drop her off. I'm good either way. Maybe we can take the girls for lunch."

Donna smiled when she felt Candace's arms encircle her neck from behind as she planted a kiss on her cheek.

"Let's see what tomorrow holds. If this night turns out the way I'm hoping it does, you'll be texting me from his bed telling me to keep Zoe an extra day. Have fun tonight and I love you."

Donna nodded.

"I will and I love you too. Let me get a hug and kiss from Zoe before you leave."

"Hurry up. We're running out the door."

Donna took her shoes off briefly and sprinted for the stairs to catch Zoe in the family room before they left. The extra pep in her step was for Clayton.

14

Life slowly seeped out of Clayton's body the closer he got to Donna's house. He wasn't ready for the date to be over. He never imagined that the only woman he's ever deeply loved would be sitting across the table from again smiling, laughing and joking as if they were long lost friends. In a sense, they were. They had a history that was unmatched to any he'd ever had with a woman. He thought that sitting across from her, he would spend the night apologizing for the past, but the moment he picked her up for their date and she opened her front door to him with a big, welcoming smile, he knew that's not what the agenda for their evening would be.

As he drove, his eyes would search her out as often as he could without causing a car crash. When they weren't chatting, he eyed her swaying in her seat to the sweet, sultry sounds of Toni Braxton an artist, that at one time, they loved every song she'd ever put out. He saw sexy, creamy thighs looking at him through the part in her dress and he found himself shifting in his own seat for a different reason. He needed to focus to hide the obvious signs of his desire for her.

"Still love Toni, I see," he uttered, smiling her way as his eyes traveled up and down her body. Everything about him had been screaming to hold her in his arms just to feel her and to know that being in her presence again was real.

"I would be lying if I said I didn't. I still listen to her music pretty much every day. There isn't much new music, these days, that I find as appealing as the music from that era. There is so much emphasis on rap that the good mood music isn't a priority for artists anymore. I miss that, so I go back to what I know.

"I know the feeling. Nothing like good music to set the mood."

When Donna looked his way, he knew that the woman sitting in the passenger seat was an entire mood herself. He wanted to be where she was.

"Are you setting the mood?" she asked.

"I think the entire night is a mood. It started when I arrived at your house to pick you up and the most beautiful woman opened the door with a smile that let me know she was as happy to see me as I was to see her. I'm not ashamed to admit that I spent the entire day checking the time. I have been counting down the time ever since you said yes to having dinner with me. Over dinner, we talked about so many things, but not about the fact that we are on a date," he said.

"Did we need a separate discussion about being on a date or should be just go with the fact that we are on a date and I'm having the best date that I've had in a long time?"

"Even a few Fridays ago?" he asked.

"What?"

He'd led the cat out of the bag and he knew it. He had to come clean.

"I saw you at the grand opening of Club Tremble."

"You were there, too?"

"I was. The owner is a good friend of mine."

"The ex-boxer is your friend?"

"I performed life-saving surgery on him after an accident he had in Vegas. We've been good friends since then."

"You saw me and didn't say hello?"

"I didn't want to intrude. You were on a date with someone. I was actually jealous of him, but don't tell anyone," Clayton joked.

"I'm telling everybody! Clayton Myers was jealous of another man? Nonsense. That's gossip blog worthy information."

Clayton laughed along with her. She was right. He wasn't known for a jealous streak. That was until he came face to face with his past and his goal was getting her back into his life. She just didn't know it yet.

Before he could respond, a song came on and breathed even more life into Donna. She wasn't only swaying, she was practically dancing around in her seat to a song by Kendrick Lamar.

"Okay, maybe there are a few rap artists that I like. I love everything by Kendrick Lamar!"

"I should have taken you dancing. You are giving that seat a workout. Perhaps on our next date we can hit up Club Tremble together, unless your dance card is already full."

"Let me address that elephant right now. His name is Lance and I'm not dating him. My sister set me up with him. He is friends with a guy I thought she was dating, but I think he was only some kind of booty call. It looks like she's getting back with her husband. I still love to dance and in between stories about his ex-girlfriend, he was actually a good dance partner. I didn't go out with him again. I would love to go out with you again, especially if dancing is involved."

"Two dates? I'm on a roll!" he added as he pulled up and parked in front of her house. He was already sad that the date was almost over.

"Maybe I'll be the lucky one and there will be a third," she said.

Keeping his eyes forward, he knew that they had been flirting with each other all night. There were several times that he'd reached across the table to link his fingers with hers. As they kept their eyes on each other, he felt her finger caressing his hand. His body was still on fire for her. He needed a cold shower immediately.

He was about to open his car door to escort her to

the front door when he felt a light tap on his arm. Turning, his heart did flips at the way Donna was gazing at him. Her head was tilted slightly to the right and though her face didn't sport a bright smile, she wasn't frowning either. Her eyes were telling him a story and if he was correct in what he saw, they were in the same part of the novel where desire was about to control their next move. Did he dare ask about the story her eyes were telling? He could be wrong, but he's been wrong before.

"I..I just wanted to tell you that I had a really good time tonight. I thought it would be awkward, but then I remembered that from the moment you asked me to have dinner with you, I had never wanted to have dinner with anyone before as much as I wanted to with you. I wanted you to know that before you walked me to my door. Thank you for a wonderful evening."

Clayton opened his mouth to respond, but changed his mind from the words that were on his lips but not on his heart. He had no right to ask for anything, but he was about to, even if it meant putting his foot in his mouth and living through an embarrassing moment.

"I'm glad you said yes when I asked. Tonight, was everything I hoped it would be. Did you enjoy the food?" he asked.

Donna beamed at him.

"I know you had Will fix my favorite dish. That was not a coincidence and it wasn't even on the menu. How did you know I still loved crab cakes? Also, there was something familiar about those crab cakes. Should I even ask?"

Clayton chuckled knowing he had been found out.

"I called Will and asked him to lay out the red carpet for this date. He didn't know all of our history but he knew you were special. I asked him if he would be able to order crab cakes from Baltimore and he got right on it. He ordered them last night, late, and they came in today, next day air. Adding in his own flavor to the lamb chops and veggies, the meal was already on its way to perfection. The only necessity to take the night beyond perfection was to add you into the mix."

"No! He ordered from Pappas in Baltimore?"

"Yes. They shipped them and all he had to do was cook them."

"You went all out."

"You noticed."

"I noticed everything about tonight," she said.

Clayton noticed everything too. What he was noticing at this moment was how breathy Donna's words were getting. She was nervous and excited. He had a feeling that like him, she didn't want the night to end. They could have had this conversation at the door, but she wanted it now.

"Everything?" he asked.

He wanted her to be able to read his desire on his face before he spoke it. He needed more than his words; he needed her to read the feelings he was emitting her way in the car. Nothing may happen between them and he would be okay with that. He couldn't deny that he wanted to see her again and again and again. Could he be entitled to her attention on more than one date? Did he dare ask?

Donna's eyes dropped from his eyes to her lap for a few seconds before she turned back and locked eyes with him again.

"Honesty?" she asked.

"Yes, please," he responded.

"I see you, Clayton. I did the moment we saw each other at the girls' camp. I know your look. Seeing you look at me like you've looked at me all evening took me back. My mind went back to your Hopkins days, not the bad times, but the really good times. Then I let go of all of that and focused on the here and now and what that look means today."

"Well, I hope you know it means that I know we have a past that was rocky, but today is a new day. We've both had lives over the years, but right here and right now, it's you and me. I couldn't have asked for fate to have played a better hand in life for me than what I'm experiencing right now. I don't know what it all means, but damn, I will not shoo away a gift; that gift is you. Can you see that I still desire you? Am I wrong for still wanting you? Do I even deserve to?"

When Donna put her hand up to stop him, he quieted.

"Don't. I don't ever want you to think that you aren't worthy of me or the other way around. We are here and that's all that matters. Every single time that you ask me out on a date, the answer is yes under one condition."

"That would be?"

"No more talk of the past. What happened is done. No more living back there. Whatever that was for each of us still led us here. I am not a believer in coincidence, but I do believe in fate."

"Okay, I have a request also."

"I'm all ears."

"Openhearted too?" he asked.

"Yes."

"I agree to your terms of leaving the past in the past after I say this one last thing and then I'm done. I apologize for not seeing your worth like I should have. I was young, stupid and operating outside of my heart. I have discovered that a love like what we had doesn't happen to everyone and I took it for granted. I can honestly say I never found it again. I want to date you and show you the man I am today. I didn't think I'd ever be here knowing that it should have been you all along that I gave my all to. I don't know what the future holds, but if I have any chance at all of one with you, I want that more than anything. I know we've only been on one date, but we're not strangers who just met. What we need to do is see who we are and can be to each other now, if you're open to that."

He didn't know what to expect, but hesitation was not a part of his personality. He was reaching for the possibility of everything good. He let her walk out of his life once before. He was being given a chance to make right from a wrong.

When Donna's hand reached up to caress his face, he turned into it and kissed her hand. He'd done it on instinct and from a desire so deep for her that having her touch him anywhere was all he could ask for. That one kiss turned into a second and then a third. She'd told him that she could see him. He wanted her to really see him as he leaned toward her slowly, giving her enough time to pull away if that's what she wanted to do. It wasn't. Donna leaned toward him and in the next moment, their lips touched for a quick kiss. From that, the fireworks began. He went back in for more, but not soft and innocent like the first. He moaned out his pleasure of knowing they longed for each other. His insides clenched with a powerful need that removed all sense of time outside of this moment.

He inhaled at the edge of her lips and took in the sweet, smokey smell of her perfume as the fragranced danced in his nostrils. When his lips captured hers and she returned the feast on his lips that he was lavishing on hers, it was sexy, it was spicy it was saucy and it was all Donna.

Pulling her as close to him as he could, he flicked his tongue from the bottom of her lower lip to the top of her upper one. He searched out her tongue and the glide across her was like lightening shooting across his brow. He wasn't getting enough. He needed so much more. He drank from her and when she moaned her own pleasure at the intimate intertwining, he gave them room to breathe right before getting a little more until the need to breathe interrupted their coupling. Fire! The kiss was all fire! As it ended and Clayton felt the emptiness that followed, he struggled to get through the next moment without tasting more of her. He smiled realizing they were both out of breath and gasping for air. His eyes lasered in on her lips and the thoroughly kissed way they called to him. He was starving for her. Her heated gaze matched his. When she leaned back toward him again, he knew her hunger matched his.

"We could take this inside, you know. How nosey are your neighbors?" he quipped.

Donna looked around forgetting that they were sitting in the car devouring each other.

"I don't know. I haven't been here long enough to know anyone yet. I don't see any blinds moving or curtains swaying. Taking this inside is the second-best idea you've had after asking me out. Shall we?" she asked.

Clayton didn't wait another second before stepping out of the car and walking around to help her out. When she exited the car and sidled up to him, he had hoped he could wait until they were inside to kiss her again, but he couldn't.

Shutting her car door, he pulled her flush against his body. When her lips curved into a sexy smile, he leaned down and kiss the smile, not caring that anyone could see them. The only thing that mattered was the woman in his arms and making sure she never felt an ounce of doubt of letting him back into her life. Her eyes sparkled. He couldn't look or move away.

When his lips found hers again, they were still slick with the essence of the first kiss in the car. His pulse rushed as Donna took his lips in a possessive kiss. He let her have total control. It was clear she wanted him to feel her the way he wanted her to feel him.

As their lips once again familiarized themselves, Clayton reached his hand to the nape of Donna's neck as his fingers found a soft grip within the long tendrils of her hair. When Donna's hands reached around him, pulling him closer to her, the action blindsided him. There was no doubt she could feel his desire for her pressing hard and ready between them and yet, she sought out more of him. He wished he were about to control his body's reaction to her, but he wasn't ashamed. He knew this wasn't the time, but his heart was in control of his mind and body; all wanted Donna.

When he pulled back and searched her eyes, thunderous passion greeted him. They stood there, no words, no movement.

"Okay, I think we are officially giving my neighbors a show."

Taking her hand, he walked them to the front door. More kissing awaited him inside.

15

Once inside, he glanced around as lights illuminated the large expanse of her entryway. He couldn't help taking a quick glance into her living room as he heard the ding of her home alarm disarming.

"Wow! Your house, the parts I can see, is very nice. I guess you're officially still moving in from the tons of boxes I see. You know I can help with that, if you like."

When he turned expecting Donna to respond, he stopped dead in his tracks. His tongue felt like lead in his mouth. If he ever thought back over his life to a time when he was the luckiest man alive, this was it.

Donna had not moved from the door where he left her. In fact, she was now leaning back against it. She had dropped her bag to the floor and with eyes planted solidly on him, he couldn't tear his gaze away from her hands. They were reaching for the tie on the side of her dress which kept it together. His mouth went dry the moment he watched her release the tie as the soft blue material parted giving him a front row seat of what was underneath. He knew she was perfection and now she was showing him just how much. Pushing the material to the side as her hands found her waist, his eyes landed on a matching blue, satin-like bra that barely held her large breasts. They peaked out at him and like a moth to a flame, he couldn't tear himself away.

Without saying a word, his eyes traveled down her body to a flat stomach that spoke of a woman who was serious about being in shape. He remembered that about her. Her body was much fuller and shapelier and he loved it. She was tantalizing him. With eyes that wouldn't stop traveling, they landed on a silky, matching pair of panties with a cute little silver bow on each side of her curvy hips. When his eyes settled on her perfectly toned legs, his mind went to a vision of those legs wrapped tight around as he joined them again and again. Was he really seeing her loving and desirable before him or was he experiencing a dream coming to reality? When he looked to her face, the sexy smile on her face told him that she knew she had him in every way that mattered.

"I was hoping you might be interested in unpacking more than just a few moving boxes. Up to you or am I being too forward?"

She wasn't even nervous. Donna relayed all confidence is the tantalizing vixen she knew she was. The sexy tone of her voice played havoc with his restraint. There was no way she had any inkling of the impact she had on him standing before him looking like a goddess. He couldn't find any words that sounded like he was an intelligent doctor with years of education under his belt. He only had one word.

"Damn!" he shouted. "Okay, that's what was under that dress all night? I won't lie and say I wasn't imagining, but again, damn!"

"Too much? Too soon? I just thought that there was a chance that we were dancing around this all night. I know I was. The way you were kissing me, I wasn't sure I could dance around this the rest of the evening. I thought about offering you some coffee or offering an invitation to watch a movie or perhaps play a board game. Truth is, I don't have any coffee, I don't want to watch television and board games are for kids," she chuckled.

Finally finding the strength to move, he walked over to her within a whisper of her lips, poked out and ready for him.

"Too much? Hell no. Have you seen yourself? I mean, damn, Donna. You are trying to kill a brother," he whispered close to her lips. He could feel the minty, heated breath from her mouth against his lips when she exhaled. "Are you sure?" he asked.

"Are you?" she countered.

Clayton wasn't one to play games and from what he could remember, neither was she. To prove his point without words, he took her hand and placed it on his hardness between them, making sure to move their hands together up and down to give her the full impact of him seeing her open and ready for him. When he stilled his own hand which rested on top of hers, her movement up and down him continued. He leaned close to her ear, allowing his tongue to slide over the lobe before he sucked it into his mouth. When he heard a sexy mewl come from her mouth, he knew he had hit the jackpot. As ready as he obviously was for her, she was just as heatedly excited for him.

"You know, I'm not a big coffee drinker. Tonight, there is something more enticing and important than movies. Lastly, I have my own version of board games that we can play, but instead of a board, they involve a bed, the wall, these steps, damn near any surface that I can get you on. How's that for a response now that more blood has gathered back in my brain?"

Not letting her respond, he didn't really need an answer. He only needed her. From the way she was gripping and caressing him through his pants, she needed him too.

Taking both of her hands. He raised them above her head, holding them there as his lips caressed the side of her face, moving around to her lips. His mind was foggy with desire. Had he ever wanted a woman this much? He knew the answer was no. This is how life was always supposed to be.

Taking her lips, he pressed against her body just enough to give them both a hint of what was in store for them. Moving his hips as slight as he could, he moved against her as she moaned into his mouth. He knew what she was going through. He felt it too.

His pulse quickened and the kiss deepened as they kissed each other with as much pent-up energy as two people could gather who, to him, had been longing for this moment for a long time. He had and his plan was to make sure Donna got all that she sought the moment she opened her dress and looked at him with eyes that sexily conveyed what her need was; him.

Moving from her lips, his own lips found the perfect spot on her sexy, sleek neck. From the way Donna was moving with a slow grind against him, he was on the right path. The sound of their breathing edged him on. He knew where they wanted to be, but he wanted them to enjoy the path to getting to the ultimate ride. He'd longed and dreamed about this moment for too long to get to it in haste.

"More," Donna said hazily and he gave her just that.

Reaching for her dress, he slid it from her body and watched, as if in slow motion, it cascaded down her body, landing in a heap at her feet. He smiled when she kicked it away as if it were something foreign that she didn't want to have anything to do with. He knew the feeling. At this point, clothes were irrelevant.

Clayton kissed the area between her breasts as he reached behind her, undoing the snap of her bra in less than a second. He was like a kid in a candy store the minute the blue cups fell away and into his hands fell the most beautiful example of pure womanhood he'd ever held. The weight and feel of them felt like home. Holding them, pushing them close together, he made sure his mouth gave equal attention to each as Donna squirmed more feverishly against the door. He needed her naked. He needed to be naked.

Picking her up, he thought about racing up the stairs with her in his arms, but instead, decided to put them out of their misery as quick as he could. They had all night to roll around in her bed finding great use of his knowledge of the Kama Sutra. Scandalous positions were his favorite thing.

He moved them to the carpeted steps, resting her body across his thighs with her legs spread. He could smell her arousal. He wanted her to know he could. Leaning forward, he rubbed his nose across the thin layer of her panties as he inhaled sharply. Surprising her, he replaced his nose with his tongue causing Donna to leap, almost out of his grasp. Finding a large amount of moisture there before his tongue even touched her, his body stoked a fire within him that could be doused only when their bodies were connected. Knowing his fully clothed body was a hinderance, he stood, keeping his eyes on hers. With the speed of light, he removed every piece of clothing he had on, almost toppling over to get his pants off. He couldn't remember a time that he'd disrobed this fast. The action even sent Donna into a fit of laughter. He laughed with her at how anxious he was.

"It's your fault. You can't just open your dress on

an unsuspecting brother and think that he wouldn't break a bone to get out of his clothes to get to you."

He watched her eyes as they traveled to that part of him that he was ready to bring her the desire she wanted from him. When she licked her lips, he shook his head at her.

"There will be time for that later. I swear if I don't get inside of you, I'm going to drop dead right here in your entryway."

"Well, as a doctor, I would revive you enough to finish the job. No half-stepping – not tonight. This has been a long time coming," she replied humorously.

They each heard the word and he couldn't agree more. That's exactly the plan for them.

"I've missed you something terrible," he admitted, rejoining her back on the stairs where he reached for the ties at her hips, pulling on one string as the material fell away, leaving her in nothing but her high heels. He wanted those on.

Clayton leaned in to kiss her and she stopped him.

"I have missed you too. It sounds irrational hearing you say it as much as it does to hear me say it, but it's the honest to goodness truth. I have missed you."

"I'm here, now, baby. I'm here now. You have my full, complete, undivided attention. Tell me what you need," he whispered close to her lips.

"You. I need you, Clayton. I need you."

When Donna opened her legs further across his thighs, he braced himself on the step that was second to the bottom. He already knew the ride would not only be pleasurable, but a rocky one. He wouldn't be able to contain the lust and desire that burned inside of him for her.

Reaching between them, he ran his finger across her now naked and moist womanhood. Finding her more than ready for him, he made sure their gazes were completely focused on each other.

"There is so much I want to do to you and with you. I promise I will get to all of that, but it's been like a dream touching and kissing you again. I just want to feel you."

"Yes!" Donna exclaimed.

Before his next breath in, Clayton gripped himself and moved ever so slowly into her body, giving her a little bit of him at a time. When her body gripped him, his teeth clamped together as he fought the desire to surge forward. He moved his hips in and out, around and around, taking great care with her as she pulled his body closer to hers. Slipping his arms under her legs to brace them, he leaned in and accepted the kiss she planted on him. As he moved, the only sounds in the room were of them breathing, racing to secure the loving they had both missed out on.

"Baby," he uttered against her lips as he found a slow and methodical rhythm that they enjoyed. Donna matched his lovemaking, getting everything she needed. As her arms went up and circled his neck, his strokes turn to long, powerful ones.

"Yes, yes, yes!" Donna screamed.

Her cries of pleasure pushed him forward. He didn't want to hurt her in the position they were in on the steps. He could feel sweat forming on his brow as he used all the strength in him to control his movement.

"Jeez!" he hollered, leaning down until his head was in the crook her space between Donna's head and her shoulder. He let his hips do the work.

"Don't hold back. I know what you're doing. You won't hurt me. I want all of you. You feel so good. I promise you won't hurt me," Donna begged.

Clayton leaned up, still with her legs braced on his arms, he planted his feet on the floor, raised himself up and with a brazen determination, he gave her all of his power. With her hands caressing him all over, the moment she gripped his shoulders, digging her nails in, his meticulous, precise strokes drove them both mad with desire.

He caught sight of Donna in the throes of the ultimate pleasure. Her eyes closed and her head tossed from side to side. She still held to him. Her hips raised up to meet him thrust for thrust. When her mouth opened and a piercing yelp hit his ears, he knew what was happening. He kept up the pace. He enjoyed watching her the moment her release took her to another dimension. His teeth chattered. He tried his best to hold on to the last vestiges of his own release that threatened to overtake him. He needed to see her.

He'd dreamed of being with her like this. Seeing the enjoyment she was experiencing meant everything to him.

"Clay!" Donna yelled.

That was all he needed. His resolve melted away. His body gave in as he reached down, grabbed her hips and allowed his orgasm to drain every bit of strength he had. He allowed himself to love her freely, holding nothing back. His body bucked and the animalistic growl heard in the air was his own. He didn't care, they rose together, taking advantage of the enjoyment. With his mind turned to mush and his body on fire, Clayton surged into her two times before his body quaked uncontrollably. He was losing his grip on her hips. His body wracked out of control, in a frenzy of unadulterated pleasure. He rode out the magnitude of his climax while the sound of their bodies caressed his body on even further. When he should have been preparing his body's calming to take place, Donna's increased strokes pushed him on further. He felt it as his eyes opened and caught a glimpse of her. She was in the middle of a second orgasm. He knew he couldn't stop now. Lowering her legs, he continued to give her all of him. He delighted in the way she rode through her second wave, reaching the apex as her yells filled the air around them; music to his ears.

"That's it, baby! That's it! I feel you. I feel you and you feel amazing. Yes, baby!" he crooned against her ear. When her body slumped back against the steps, he laid on her chest. He felt her struggling to calm her breathing. Hearing her heart beating rapidly against his cheek was the most perfect sound in the world. He wanted to say something in the moment, but controlling his breath was going to take a few moments while his body calmed.

He reached down and caressed Donna's legs and hips where he knew he'd held them in a death grip.

"How are we going to explain the love bruises," Donna joked, reaching for him and holding him tight in her arms.

"I'm going to say that you put a brother through a serious workout, one worth every second. Am I really still breathing?" he joked.

"Are we still breathing? What the hell was that experience? Two?"

"Yeah, I felt both of them. I loved watching you – you were almost angelic."

"I don't know if that's the word I would use, but I'll give you that. Everything about what we just did was beyond sinful – the *good* kind!"

When Donna stiffened under him, he moved, thinking his weight was too heavy.

"What's wrong? Am I heavy?" he asked.

"No. I feel you getting hard inside of me again. Are you serious, right now?"

Clayton laughed so hard, he had to sit up to avoid getting a cramp.

"It's what you do to me. Shall we take this to a bed

now?"

"Only if you give carrier service because I don't think my legs will work."

Clayton reached for her, lifting her effortlessly. The excitement of what was to come gave him he-man strength. He was ready.

**

Daylight hit Donna in the face. She woke, immediately snapping her body straight up. She hardly ever slept in, even on her day off. Her brain was still foggy at the early morning hour. She wondered if Zoe had gotten up and already fixed cereal. She was surprised her ball-of-fire daughter hadn't come in and jumped on her bed to wake her up. Then it happened. A strong hand came around and caressed her arm. She then remembered. She wasn't alone and Zoe wasn't at home. She was in bed and she wasn't alone; Clayton was in bed with her. It hadn't been a dream. She'd spent the whole night having mind-blowing sex in so many positions that she lost count around five in the morning. She'd had more sex the night before than she'd had in the past couple of years. When reality hit her, she felt a slight tinge of pain in her legs and even more enjoyable soreness a little further up. She turned to find Clayton's eyes still closed but his hand was trying to pull her toward him.

"You're too far away," he uttered.

"For a second, I forgot what reality was. I'm used to jumping up to find out what Zoe is doing. I forgot she isn't here."

"I'm here," he replied.

Donna moved back until she was again under the thin blanket and cocooned in Clayton's tight embrace. They were face-to-face and now, eye-to-eye. She whimpered with a hunger for him, remembering all they had shared.

"Good morning," she slurred. Accepting the kiss that Clayton moved forward to give her, she reached under the blanket and hugged his body, pulling herself even closer.

"Good morning to you. I thought you woke with regret that I was here. You sat up so fast, I didn't know what to think."

"Well, I haven't slept this good in a long time. You put me to sleep and when I woke, I realized this must be what it feels like to come out of a coma," she jested.

"We put each other to sleep even if it was only for a few hours. I remember seeing that clock on your nightstand reading about five in the morning when we were finally drifting off with you in my arms. That was perfection at its best. Correction, having you like this in the light of day is perfection. Pinch me so that I know you're real."

When she did, he winced.

"Ouch," he declared.

Donna kissed the spot where she'd pinched him.

"Better?" she asked.

"Yes and no because I liked it."

This time, Donna kissed him on the lips. It wasn't

a small peck on the lips, but she needed to revisit the feeling of the night before. There was no regret or doubt about them being together. She went into this knowing what she wanted.

"You were perfect. I do believe we were perfect together. I've never had that kind of sexual experience in my life. There were more acrobatics than in a circus."

She watched Clayton bang on his chest like Tarzan and she almost choked she laughed so hard.

"I did my best to come through. Remember, I want a second date with you. The more I felt you enjoying yourself, the further I took our lovemaking. Have no doubt, it gets even better. That's what this was, you know – not just sex – it was lovemaking."

She was thinking the same thing. Holding him even tighter, she nodded her head.

"Yes, it was and it was amazing."

"What now? I know things went pretty fast after one date," Clayton asked her.

"More?" she asked.

"Woman, that was the best first date of my entire existence. I can't wait to see what you have planned for me after our second date!"

"You want to wait for the second date when I've got time this morning?" she asked.

"You're not kicking me out yet?" he asked.

"I am completely in my right mind. I would never do anything that foolish!" she declared confidently.

In response, she giggled when Clayton effortlessly

lifted her, placing her in a straddle position across his waist.

"I say let's not let the morning go to waste. We can talk about what's next for us later."

"Am I too presumptuous if I say, I want to leap feet first into a relationship with you – no other dating? Is that too much? Am I now moving too fast?"

Donna beamed at him knowing she would like nothing more.

"I don't know. I think I need a little more convincing, if you're up for that."

She looked beneath the blanket.

"Looks like you are!" she giggled.

"Challenge issued and accepted. I can do that," he said.

When he quickly flipped them, placing her under him, she let him do just that.

16

Donna sat in her office at the hospital across from, Carlotta Olmos, Jack's mother. Absent from this meeting, unlike the others, was Carlotta's husband, Emilio. They had been meeting at least once a week to discuss Jack's case. The decision was made that he was going to need a transplant as both of his kidneys lost their function. For the meeting that was set up for both parents later in the day, Donna was surprised that she'd received a call that Carlotta wanted to speak with her without her husband present.

As they spoke of options for Jack when it came to the best possible donors, she watched the color of Carlotta's face turn to a gray paste like tone.

"Dr. Spencer, I appreciate all that you've done for us, but there is a problem if we proceed; something I haven't told you or my husband. It's bad; it's really bad."

Carlotta shook uncontrollably. Donna was beyond concerned; she was frightened.

"What is it? The meeting we were to have together later today was when I was going to get you set up for your blood work-up and other tests to determine if you or Emilio would be a good match as a donor for Jack. You're still planning to do that, right? Jack won't survive without a transplant. Of course, he's being moved to the top of the list because of the downward turn his condition has taken, but the best course here may be one of you. What's the issue?" she asked.

Before Carlotta could respond, Donna's cell phone buzzed on her hip. She had been waiting on a call from Clayton and she needed to take his call.

"You can take that. It'll give me a few minutes to gather my thoughts," Carlotta said.

"This will only take a moment. Stay here in my office. I'm going to step into one of the exam rooms."

Exiting the room and seeking some privacy, she smiled the moment she heard Clayton's voice on the other end. They'd been secretly dating for a month, keeping it to themselves before they told anyone, especially their daughters. The month had been filled with so much joy, just the mere thought of him gave her pleasure.

"Hey you!" Clayton gleefully greeted her.

"Hey yourself. I was thinking about you."

"Good because I'm always thinking about you. I'm sorry I'm just getting back to you. I had two surgeries today. When I came out, my assistant said you had called. How is my sexy girlfriend doing? I love the sound of those words every time I say them.”

“Mmm, they sound good to me too. I’m doing good.”

“Are you calling with an answer to my question about going to my house on the beach in a few weeks after the girls get out of camp for the summer? I didn’t know if you thought that was a bad idea considering we haven’t told anyone about us. I have to admit that I told Sebastian and Patrick. Of course, Will knows because of that dinner we had.”

Donna exhaled. She was glad she wasn’t the only one who couldn’t keep a secret.

“You know my sister knows. The morning after that first night at my house, that was her calling to see if it was safe to bring Zoe home.”

“Is that what you were responding to when you hopped out of bed before we took that incredible shower together? All I could hear you saying was no and then you hung up. That was Candace?”

“That was her. She read me the third degree for the rest of the day until I told her that the coast wasn’t clear because you were in bed next to me. She danced around like a child for the rest of the day. She’s more excited for me and you than we are.”

“That’s not possible. I’m having the time of my life with you. I admit, it’s getting tricky finding time to spend together without feeling like a bad parent for not telling Brooklyn and Zoe. One day, we’re going to have to tell them that I’m in love with you.”

"And that I'm in love with you, too. Our girls are inquisitive," Donna admitted.

"Oh, you have no idea. Brooklyn is a little spy. She told me the other day that I seem happier to her; like I have a happy secret. She has no idea!" he quipped.

"Speaking of them – I called you to ask if you could pick up Zoe when you pick up Brooklyn. I hate to ask with such short notice, but I have a parent who changed the time of a meeting with me today and I think it's going to be a deep conversation. Something tells me she's holding onto secrets of her own that she's about to tell me. Benny is out of town and her grandparents are just getting back from a trip. I could call my sister if you can't."

"Baby, slow down. Yes, I can do that. I would do anything for you. I'm actually heading out a little early today. I was planning to check out early and play a few rounds of golf, but now, I don't even feel like doing that. My body is tired. I did interviews for a second in command chief of surgery and that was exhausting."

"Aw, my baby. I wish I was with you to rub you down and take that pain away."

"I'm going to hold you to that, most definitely. I love your definition of rubbing me down. I've never picked up Zoe before. You'll have to call and notify the camp. Why don't you add me as a pickup or drop-off for Zoe and I'll do the same with Brooklyn? If either of us is ever in a bind, we can have each other's backs. Are you going to be late? I could put a few hot dogs and burgers on the grill for them and throw on a couple of movies. Don't feel like you have to rush to pick Zoe up."

Donna still pinched herself daily wondering how she could be so blessed as to have a wonderful man like Clayton loving everything about her.

"Have I told you today how much I love you?" she asked.

Clayton never thought he'd hear her say those words ever again. Each time she says them, his heart swells a little more.

"You sent me a text early this morning letting me know you love me and I love you too, baby. I'm excited that I get to see you tonight. I haven't seen you in a few days and I need my fill."

"The girls will be there."

"We can sneak away into a closet for a quick peck on the lips. I need it. You're making a brother go through withdrawals."

"I got you covered; you know that. As far as the beach, my answer is yes. Zoe will be going away the week after that with her father on a trip to Florida, so that will be a fun time for her and Brooklyn. She'll love coming back home to repack to go on another trip right after that one. How will we explain that?" she asked.

Donna had thought about nothing more than how to spend quality time with Clayton if she agreed to the trip to the beach for a week. She needed time off just as he did, but they weren't quite ready for the girls to know about them yet.

"We'll figure it out. We can put Zoe and Brooklyn in the room with bunkbeds. You'll have your own room and so will I. Sebastian is coming with a friend who has kids around our girls' ages. I'm also bringing my babysitter along. If there is an emergency of any kind and I need to get back to the hospital, she'll be there to look after Brooklyn so that I don't interrupt her vacation time. My child is a fish when it comes to water. She's been begging for a pool at the house. I'm planning to have an in-ground pool added next summer."

"That sounds nice. Zoe loves to swim, too. She's been taking lessons since she was a baby. On this trip, will we have any time alone? A whole week and we have to abstain?"

Donna was already struggling with the lack of time they get to spend together due to their busy schedules. To go away on a vacation and not have time alone would be pure torture.

"We'll figure it out. I'm not planning on being away with you for an entire week and not be able to touch, kiss and make love to you. I like that we can find time in the middle of the day sometimes to sneak around, but in the same house for an entire week, we'll have to work something out."

"It wouldn't be so bad if our lovemaking wasn't as loud and wild, you know, like we both like. We would wake the dead in that house!"

"You mean you!" Clayton countered.

"I mean us! Zoe and I are in. I've put in for the time

off, which is a part of any contract I've ever had with a hospital. I always take time right before Zoe goes back to school in order to take a vacation. She's going with Benny this year, something he has never done. I still kept my usual two weeks."

"So that means that I can see you that week? My parents are coming up that last week before school to spend it with Brooklyn. They'll keep her busy. I love the idea of sneaking out of the house to see you."

"Me too. I'll call the camp right now to let them know they can release Zoe to you. I'm sure they'll ask me to email that over in writing, so I'll get ahead of them and do that."

"Listen, you may want to tell Benny about us. What if he finds out my name is the card to pick up Zoe when you have an emergency and he's not available? Does he know who I am?"

Donna exhaled loudly. She hadn't thought about that.

"He doesn't know we're seeing each other but he does know who you are from my past. You're right that I need to tell him. I will. Thanks for suggesting it. I guess our small circle of people we're telling is getting bigger."

"Is that a problem for you?" Clayton asked.

"Not at all. I love you and that's what matters."

"I'll let you go and get back to what you were doing. I love you, baby. I love you," Clayton expressed.

She could hear the words as if they were spoken

from his heart and not just his mouth.

"I love you, too. I'll see you later. Make sure you find that closet," she joked and then raced back to Carlotta.

When she entered her office, she found her standing at the window looking out over the parking lot.

"Carlotta? Are you okay? Come sit down. Let's talk."

"Dr. Spencer, I'm in a bind. Who knew Jack would have medical problems that would be this bad? I never expected anything like this. Listen, I can't let Emilio go through the testing. Can you just test me? Maybe I'm a perfect match and we won't need Emilio."

Donna had an idea of where the conversation was going and she didn't like it.

"Carlotta, you have to tell me what's going on. I'm Jack's doctor and he is my priority."

"I don't know if I can. I'm saying, if you can just have me tested and if I'm a match, we won't need Emilio. Isn't that a possibility? What about someone else who might be a match? Aren't there thousands of donors all the time? Does it have to be me or Emilio? I can't have him go for the test. If he does and things don't turn out, it could ruin my marriage. I'm begging you to please just test me and leave Emilio out of this."

"What would you tell him when he's not tested? He's going to ask why. I'm asking you to trust me right now and tell me what's going on."

Donna leaned forward on her haunches and waited. She needed to push Carlotta because whatever was going on with her, getting Jack a kidney was what mattered. First, they needed to get through whatever was bothering her.

"Okay, well, Emilio is not Jack's father. I'm afraid something will come out that shows he's not his daddy and my marriage will be over."

She knew it. This was not her first rodeo with a mother or father with questionable parentage.

"Why are you just telling me this? Start from the beginning."

"I didn't think we would get to the point that you would need blood from me or Emilio. There was a month when Emilio was locked up in jail and I messed around with a friend. I was lonely. I found out I was pregnant and I knew it wasn't Emilio when the doctor gave me my due date. When I was with Emilio again, I was already pregnant. I lied to him when I gave birth and told him that Jack came early. He wasn't there with me when I gave birth, so it was easy to lie. Then Jack got sick and his kidneys began failing. Now, he needs a transplant and you're saying that the best possible options are me and Emilio. He can't know that he's not Jack's father. We tried for two years to get pregnant and nothing. He was so happy when I told him I was pregnant. He can't know. It will drive him mad. He's dangerous when he's mad. Can you make an exception? I can do your testing right now. I can tell Emilio I rescheduled the date for his test."

"What if it comes back that you're not a match? We would still test Emilio. You would have to keep covering up one lie with another lie. I know it's hard, but you have to tell him. If you're both not a match, it's fine and we can move on from there. The results are not a secret. If he wants to see them, I can't keep them from him. On record, he is Jack's father. I can't reveal this to him, but you must."

"Doc, I'm telling you, that's not a good idea. I don't know what he'll do. Did I tell you that he was in jail for pistol whipping someone for stepping on his new white sneakers? Those charges were dropped because the guy wouldn't testify. That's the only reason Emilio was let out after a month. Without that guy, there was no case because there were no witnesses willing to go against him. My husband is a live wire. I don't know what he'll do."

"Listen, Jack needs a kidney. You both wanted to be tested. I have no valid reason for not testing Emilio. The only thing that would stand out would be if the blood types didn't sync. Lots of people have the same blood type. I'm not giving you a reason to continue the deceit, but I need you to think about Jack. What if Emilio is a match?"

When Carlotta dropped her head down into her hands and began crying, Donna jumped up from her seat and joined her on the other side of the desk. She placed her arm around Carlotta feeling like the woman was carrying the weight of the world on her shoulders.

"He won't be. When I had Jack, I checked into the blood types to make sure there wouldn't be a problem. I'm type A, Emilio is type A and baby Jack is AB. He's not his father; something I already knew. I was hoping the types would match and I would never have to tell anyone. If the man who is Jack's biological father could be a match for Jack, I want him tested too. That would mean the end of my marriage and the beginning of Emilio's rage. He will be furious especially finding out that the man who is Jack's biological father is one of Emilio's best friends. He would kill him if he found out."

"Donors are anonymous. If you want this guy to be tested, you can have him come in and we can find out. I still recommend you telling Emilio. Jack is our concern, here."

"Doc, there's more to this. Hi biological father doesn't know that Jack is his son. Once Emilio got out of jail, Hector was ghost."

"Do you know how to find him?"

"I do."

"Think about Jack and then decide what your next step is. My obligation is to get him the best care. Most of all, if I can get him a kidney, that's what I'm going to do. There is a small window we're working with. I can't let your relationship problems get in the way."

"This is a mess. Have you ever been in a relationship that was messy?"

Donna thought back to what happened with Clayton and Michelle years ago. The issue wasn't the same as what Carlotta is going through, but yes, she understood being in the midst of mess and how secrets can ruin your life. Right now, the life that mattered was Jack's.

"I can't tell you what to do; I can only advise you about what's best for Jack, your son. You get that, right? Think about what we can do to make sure Jack survives. I want to test everyone I can because that little boy in pediatric intensive care deserves the best shot at life that we can give him. I can send you to the lab right now to be tested. What happens after that is up to you. What are you going to do?"

"I'm going to get my test done and then I'm going to tell Emilio the truth and hope for the best. He has to still love Jack even after I tell him the truth. He may hate me, but he loves Jack."

Donna stood and quickly signed the paper resting on her desk.

"Here is what you'll need for the lab. I'll hold onto Emilio's paperwork until after you talk to him."

She handed the papers to Carlotta and walked her out. As she watched her walk down the hallway, her shoulders slumped like a woman defeated. Thinking about her own life, Carlotta had brought back memories she wanted to leave buried. She once walked away from the man she loves because of mess in a relationship. If she could go back, she would have fought through her anger and held onto the love that was more important than her angry. Luckily, they found their way back to each other. She had hope that Emilio would be more forgiving than she had been of Clayton for his indiscretion. Jack's life may depend on it and as a doctor, she took her oath to heart. She had to save Jack's life.

**

Clayton walked into the parent waiting area where he signed both Brooklyn and Zoe out of camp. When they came running in, they were both jumping up and down like excited rabbits.

"Daddy! You're picking up Zoe too? Our counselor told us her mother gave you permission."

"Yes. Her mother is caught up with a patient and she knew I was picking you up. Hi, Zoe."

"Hi, Mr. Clayton."

"Are you girls ready to go?" he asked as they walked out.

He smiled following behind them to the car. This was his first time picking up Zoe, but not his first time watching the two interact. After the first outing of the girls going bowling, they'd had plenty other time hanging out, sometimes with him and Donna, but most time with just Donna.

"Are we going to do something fun until her mother comes? Can we get some ice cream? Can we go to the store? Can we go see a movie? I heard there's a carnival in town. Can we go to that? Daddy, you're not answering," Brooklyn poked.

"That's because you're tossing out too many questions without letting me answer. No, you can't have ice cream because you haven't had dinner yet. We can't go to the store because we're going home and taking Zoe with us. You and Zoe can have fun with all the stuff you have at the house. While all that fun is happening, I'm going to cook dinner. I thought I'd do burgers and hot dogs on the grill while you girls have fun. I don't know how long her mother will be, but until then, we'll make it work. Does that work for you?"

"Yeah! I love it! You are the best, daddy."

"Zoe?" he asked.

"Yes. I like going to your house. Brooklyn, I have my bracelet stuff in my backpack. We can make some, if you want," Zoe said.

Clayton watched them climb in the back and buckle up. After getting behind the steering wheel, he listened to them talk each other to death as he drove. He was imagining something more permanent like this involving him and Donna having the life together they were always supposed to have. His plan was to make them a family. Time would tell.

17

Clayton kept his eyes on Donna as she moved about his kitchen looking like a woman who belonged in his house. She looked like and felt like home. He tried to help her clear the dishes from the unplanned dinner that ended up including a few of his friends, but she wouldn't hear of it. She mentioned how he slaved over preparing everything and she wanted to do her part. He knew she'd had a long day at the hospital, but still, when she arrived and after saying hello to Zoe and Brooklyn, she got right to work helping with dinner and entertaining his friends.

Looking around at his friends who welcomed her into their group as if she'd always been around, there was Sebastian, who Donna already knew from their Hopkins days. Sitting around the large gray and white marble top island in the center of his kitchen was Reggie and his wife Selena. Their kids were in the family room with Zoe and Brooklyn playing board games. Thinking the night was still young when it actually wasn't, Sebastian had brought up the idea of playing a game of spades.

"Sebastian cheats," Reggie joked.

"Just because I win doesn't mean I cheat. You need to learn to be a master at spades like me."

"He cheats. Own up to it and free your mind!" Clayton joked.

The room broke out in laughter and Donna joined in. She still couldn't believe this was her life. She hadn't been around Sebastian in a long time. He welcomed her back into their fold with ease along with Clayton's other friends. She didn't know who else may know about her and Clayton. Until a few minutes ago, Reggie and Selena had no idea they were once again seeing each other. Clayton told her that he'd mentioned who she was to Reggie, but tonight, they shared that they were in love and have been seeing each other for well over a month. Everyone was excited for them and embraced her. Selena mentioned that she had never seen Clayton as happy as he has been lately. She wondered what the cause was and now that she knew, she was happy for them.

"Dinner was amazing. I'm glad Reggie called to see what you were up to before we just stopped by. The minute he heard you were grilling, he made a mad dash to pick up steaks, had me make a salad and on your doorstep is where we landed," Selena said.

"Yeah, my buddy is a master on the grill from the hamburgers to that spicy grilled chicken, to the steaks and hot dogs. No one cooks a perfect hot dog like Clay does, with just the right amount of burned edges," Sebastian boasted.

"I do what I can do, when I can do it!" Clayton bragged.

Donna watched Sebastian look toward the entrance to the kitchen before leaning in to the group. When he began to whisper, she joined them at the table.

"When are you going to tell the girls?" he whispered.

"We don't know yet," she replied looking to Clayton for reassurance.

"Are you and Zoe coming with us to the house on the beach?" Sebastian asked.

"Yes, we're going. Clayton mentioned it to me and I accepted," Donna said.

"That means you have to tell the girls. Clayton, you know Brooklyn is way beyond her age. She will figure out that something is going on between the two of you. Have you seen how the two of you ogle each other when you're together? That won't go unnoticed during a week at the beach."

"I know. I told Donna that. We plan to tell them. We just need a little more time. We want to tell them about our past and that we were involved years ago. They know we both were at Hopkins, but they don't realize that we already knew each other. The two of them didn't know we knew each other. We're working on it. We do plan to tell them before the trip, so we have some time."

"A little over a week? I don't understand the hesitation. Can you imagine their response?"

"We know," was all Clayton said, taking the heat from Donna and putting it on himself.

"Alright, so where are the cards? Let's get this game popping. It's not really that late. One game and we can call it a night."

"I think they're on the ledge of the fireplace in the family room. I remember sitting them there a few weeks ago after a game night," Clayton said.

"I'll get them," Donna offered.

Donna walked off with Clayton close behind her.

"I'm going to help her. We'll be back," he said, rushing before he could be questioned about why Donna would need help getting a deck of cards. He hoped no one saw the sneaky look on his face. He didn't care about a deck of cards. He needed a moment with his woman. The house had been full of people since she arrived from work. They haven't had even a second for a proper greeting. With the kids busy and not focused on them, this was the perfect moment to quietly slip away.

Before Donna could get very far, Clayton took her hand and walked them in the opposite direction of the steps that led down to the family room. He was thankful for the distance between the family room and his office, where he was hoping to buy them some time and get a sexy moment alone. At the door, he looked around before he moved a snickering Donna inside, closing the door behind them.

"Clayton Myers, what are you doing? You have guests."

"I don't care about them right now. I only care that you've been here all evening and I've been losing my mind needing to kiss you. I've been waiting to find a moment to steal you away. I figured, in your quest to find the deck of cards, I would distract you for a moment."

Donna went willingly into his arms as he pressed her back against the door in the darkened room. The only light came from the moon shining through the window.

Clayton's plan was to get a satisfying kiss that would get him through the night or at least until the next afternoon. They had already made plans to sneak away for an extended lunch break together. In preparation for the hour and a half they each set aside in the middle of their day, he already booked them a beautiful hotel suite, complete with a full lunch, a tray of fresh fruit and some good music to provide the mood for the time they needed together.

"We don't have long," Donna spoke softly close to his lips.

He didn't make either of them wait another second. Reaching up, Clayton pushed Donna's hair back from her face so that he could see all of her loveliness.

Moving his hand from the side of her face, he swiped it lower to her chin, lifting it so that he could have much easier access. Lowering his head, he locked his eyes, he knew were filled with his intention and kissed her full, luscious lips, quick but purposeful.

"Sweet," he said against them. Not giving her a chance to respond, he dove in again and this time, there was nothing soft or patient about their lip lock. A fierce fire ignited inside of him the moment he felt her hands grip the side of his shirt before circling his waist. Clayton took no time in pulling her snug against his body while his other hand went to her head, pulling her lips even closer to his. When he thought he was in total control of their kiss, he relinquished the control to Donna who sought it. When she sighed into his mouth, and then lightly nipped at his bottom lip, he suddenly wished he could carve out more time for a little more than a kiss.

Donna's lips took him on a ride to heaven like only she could do as her mouth mated with his in the most intimate way. Feeling highly energized by her zest, he joined her as their mouths toyed with each other in an attempt to get everything out of the few seconds they had together. Never does it seem like enough time.

This was life; this was the air he needed to breathe; this was what has been missing from his life for years – the kiss of a woman he would move heaven and hell for. All of his senses were on overdrive as the kiss turned fiery, sizzling hot and then it stopped when Donna suddenly moved away from his lips. That's when he heard it too. Someone was on the other side of the door clearing their throat again and again. Clayton already knew who the culprit was. He spoke to the door.

"Are you alone?" he asked.

"Yeah, so open the door," Sebastian demanded.

With Donna laughing from her hiding place behind him, Clayton slowly opened the door, smirking, knowing he had been caught.

"Your timing is poor, Sebastian. I mean, the worst timing in the history of mankind," Clayton crowed jokingly.

"Bro, you have no idea how sorry I am for entering at this very moment. I was sent to find out what was taking you so long to find the cards. When I didn't see you in the family room, I knew you were hiding with this pretty lady someplace. This room is the furthest from everything on this floor, so I took my chance.

"We just needed a minute," Clayton said.

"A minute? Haven't I taught you better than that!? Sebastian chortled.

He started laughing so loud that Clayton pulled him into the room to silence him.

"Are you trying to draw everyone here with your loud laugh?" he asked.

The three of them were now laughing hard, from the belly.

"I'll tell you what. It's clear the two of you need more than just a minute. I'm going to recommend we, not including you and Donna, take a trip to the ice cream parlor for some sundaes and take the kids with us. If they ask about you not going with us, we'll tell them that you and Donna are going to stay behind and finish cleaning up. You'll have an hour. Whatever you're going to do, get it done in an hour. When we get back, make sure there aren't any zippers down or hairs out of place, messed up makeup – you know what I'm saying? One hour, Clay."

Before he or Donna could answer, Sebastian had rushed out, leaving them alone once again.

"Is he serious?" Donna asked.

"More than you know."

They waited without moving to not alert anyone to where they were. Within seconds, they heard a mad rush for the front door. He knew the moment his daughter heard ice cream, she didn't have another care in the world. He and Donna would not be missed. He turned to her knowing time was of the essence.

"An hour?" she asked him, kicking her sandals in the process.

"Oh, baby, trust me, this is going to be much better than just stealing a kiss or two. Have you ever made love on a mahogany desk before?"

Donna quivered at the thought. Her heart lit up like a bright morning sky. If she did, the memory was gone. She only wanted to have memories with him.

"Never, but I'm always ready for new things, especially when it comes to you."

Clayton walked them backwards as his mouth plundered hers with intoxicating kisses that left his head spinning.

Like air to breathe, Donna accepted the untamed, ravaging kiss that reminded her that the love they had always shared, even while apart from each other, had long ago branded her as his one and only love and him as hers. Everything they were meant to be rested on the touch of their lips, the glide of their tongues and the life breathed into this very moment. When she leaned back, even in the darkened room, lit only by the moon, she could see the devilish grin on Clayton's face. She knew they would be utilizing the entire hour ahead of them.

When Clayton's large hands reached down and lifted her to a sitting position on the top, center of his desk, she gasped with anticipation just as his lips captured hers again. The fervor in which he loved her mouth had her clawing for his clothes, wanting to touch him; every part of him. She basked in knowing that her love knew his love and it was everlasting.

Clayton felt Donna struggling with his shirt. Helping her out, he reached and removed it, taking her hands and placing them on his overheated chest, made more sensitive by her soft touch.

"I can't see enough of you," Donna purred out.

Reaching, Clayton clicked on the light on his desk, giving the room a soft, yellow glow. It wasn't as bright as he would like it to be, but he didn't dare disconnect from her grasp to reach for the switch on the wall.

"That work?" he whispered against her neck.

"I need to feel you," she uttered against his scratchy beard. She loved the feel of the rough hairs. She longed to feel them in other places. They would have time to take things slow tomorrow during their midday tryst.

Clayton slid his hands along her covered thighs, kneading the flesh through them.

"Off," he said and lifted her slightly.

He watched Donna feverishly slide her pants down her legs where he then helped her remove them completely, leaving her bare from the waist down. Unzipping to free himself, he took in a long breath and held it when he felt her soft hands grip him, stroking him from tip to base.

"You know, there are days that I feel greedy for wanting to be inside of you anytime my eyes are open. I can't seem to get enough of making love to you. I need so much more of you. I want so much more with you. Am I in this alone?" he asked.

"No, sweetheart. You're never alone in your thinking. We've waited a long time to be together not even realizing we ever would be again. I desire you all day long. I ache for you when I have long days and I go home to my cold bed alone. I know we only have an hour, but I will take an hour over no time at all. Just love me. I want to be loved by you always and forever."

Clayton lifted her arms to his shoulders before lifting her body and moving her to the edge. Fusing their bodies, he advanced slowly with long, hard thrusts, feeling the sigh of relief that he was right where he wanted to be. Their tongues teased and dueled as their hips moved to a syncopated beat, reserved just for them.

He rubbed his pelvis against hers, allowing the intense friction to drive them to the ultimate pleasure of earthquake like tremors followed by a sensational release.

He kept his eyes glued to Donna's face as she glowed with the readiness of reaching paradise.

Donna struggled to breathe with the air thick with the aroma of she and Clayton joined intimately as spasms quickly overtook her. She felt the zing in her legs which shot straight to her womanhood, sending her soaring and screaming through the pleasure of it all. This she would never tire of, the sound and feel of him loving her with unending power.

The erratic change in his breathing alerted Clayton that he wasn't far behind Donna's mighty explosion. He too howled while bracing them on the desk. He needed more as his orgasm claimed him. Finding the little strength he had in his arms and legs, he lifted Donna up and into his arms, keeping them locked together, his hips still grinding fiercely and provocatively into hers. He held her tight as he moved backward toward the leather seat he knew he would find. Forcing his body down onto it without missing a beat, he knew that he and Donna were perfectly in sync when she took over;

he had to let her. He was enthralled as she slid onto him to the hilt, gripping him with each pass his body made into her body. He was on the edge of fantasy like ecstasy. He felt himself pulsating inside of her when he suddenly reached the highest peak, shattering, floating into oblivion. He surrendered to the orgasm that shook him to his core, his body rocking and quaking, lifting them from the seat with each surge. He struggled for control, but had none. He let his body do what it wanted to do.

"I love you, I love you!" he shouted as his body's reaction to his release set him free and he began to calm. Their breathing calmed to a level where speech was once again possible.

"The things you do to me should be outlawed! I think I actually floated outside of my body," Donna said. Her legs were still shaking from the magnitude of what they just experienced.

"Baby, I have missed you and this," he finally said, peppering her neck with licks and kisses.

"And I missed you just as much. We definitely need that vacation time together. I only hope I'm able to walk when we get back."

"Well, I'm not making any promises. You have me strung out on you!"

"It will be better when we don't have to do all of this sneaking. I love that we can take this time and focus on us. I've enjoyed going to the movies here and there, having nice romantic dates and fancy dinners and walking, holding hands as we walk through shopping centers enjoying ice cream cones while not really shopping. Once this becomes public, I don't want to lose any of our private time. We need this."

Clayton agreed. Not having to share their newfound love with anyone has allowed them to steal more time alone.

"I know. We won't lose anything. Being here is a miracle on its own. I wish we could just stay like this in the quietness for hours and hours, but we can't."

When Donna hit him with a sad face, he kissed her until she smiled again.

"We have the rest of our hour."

"What would you like to do?" he asked.

"Let's go sit out on one of your lounge chairs and look up at the stars. You can text Sebastian to tell him to warn us when they are on the way back. Until then, I just want to lay in your arms and dream while awake."

"What do you want to dream about?"

Clayton knew if he could make it come true for her, he would do everything in his power to make it happen.

"Being with you forever."

He beamed, happy that any time she shared a dream with him, he could help make it come true.

"See, there is another request I am more than happy to make happen. Let's get a quick wash up and then relax. I'll clean up the kitchen and the grill later tonight. I don't want to waste any of the time we have left on cleaning the house.

In her home office, Donna worried over Jack's latest test results. She'd read them again and again as if the prognosis was going to change. In the midst of it all, Carlotta was allowing her personal issues with her husband to impact the decision-making needed for Jack. She was willing to take the necessary steps with the hospital administration to take the decisions out of Carlotta's hands if she didn't respond soon with what the hospital needs for Jack's care.

She turned the page and reviewed Donna's test results again. Nothing about that had changed in the past few seconds either. She was a match to give Jack a kidney. Donna had been trying to reach Carlotta for an entire day and hasn't gotten a response. She was worried because, the day before, Carlotta was going to tell her husband that he wasn't Jack's father. She'd had a change of heart and felt the need to come clean, even if it turned out that she was a match. She believed it was the right thing to do. She would try her again after she talked to Clayton. There were only two more days left before their trip to the beach and her vacation would begin. She was looking forward to the week with everyone on the beach, but most of all, she was looking forward to the second week where she was on vacation. Zoe would be with Benny in Florida and she and Clayton, who decided to take an additional week of vacation, were planning an island getaway, plans she'd spent all day making. She couldn't wait to tell him all about it. She had a few loose ends to tie up at the hospital with the team who will monitor Jack closely. If he needs the surgery before she gets back, she knew all bases would be covered. She needed Carlotta and her husband at that meeting.

She was about to call her again when Clayton decided to call.

"Hey! I was thinking about you," she said, answering.

"You were? Great minds think alike because you've been on my mind all day. What's the news on our special trip away together? I'm already more excited than a kid in a candy store."

"I love when you get excited. That means all good things for me too," Donna kidded.

She was just as excited as he was.

"While I'm pulling up the itinerary, you'll be happy to know something else."

"That would be?"

"I talked to Benny about us earlier today. He

wanted to pick Zoe up and have dinner with just her. After camp, she ran to get a shower and change her clothes for their daddy and daughter date, giving me some time to tell him. I told him we've been seeing each other for a month and a half."

"What was his reaction?" Clayton asked her.

"His exact words were, he was happy that I was back with the third person in our marriage."

"What does that mean?"

Donna was hesitant to tell him the meaning behind Benny's words. Back when she was married to him, they had several arguments about Clayton, something she's never shared with anyone. Now was the time to share.

"I already told you the circumstances under which Benny and I got married. I told him what I went through. Once we were married, there was always something missing between him and me. We were married and going through the motions of being married, but we were never really in love. We leaned on each other for comfort, but love never surfaced. Anytime we had an argument about how cold we were to each other, he blamed it on what he believed to be my love for you that I had never let go of. After it all, he said my heart had always belonged to you; he saw you as the third person in our marriage. He blamed my love for another man as the reason why I couldn't open myself up to loving him."

"Donna, I'm sorry. Like you, that was the issue in

my marriage, though we didn't word things like Benny did. I'm sorry that others were hurt, but we can't go back."

"I know and he said that. He even shared that as much as he loves Alicia, he believes some of their issues are about his lack of trusting that she truly, deeply loves him. I felt so bad for him. He did share that they're going for counseling because he wants to be a better husband and father. He was really happy that you and I found each other again. I told him how it happened and he was as stunned as we were. Bottom line is, he's happy and wished us all the love and happiness in the world."

"Wow. That's amazing. Maybe there will be healing all around. I still need to talk to Michelle. I'll do it after we come back for that one day before we fly out of here. As for Brooklyn and Zoe, we're still telling them Friday evening, the night before we head to the beach? That's a day away. Are you ready?"

Donna was more than ready. She and Clayton had talked a lot lately about their family dynamic and how much he wanted to talk about what forever looked like for them. She was ready for that discussion as well.

"Yes, I'm ready. You know we can't leave here without them knowing. Since we're spending the night at your house, unbeknownst to them, that will be the perfect chance to sit them down. Zoe already knows she's spending the night and going with you, but she doesn't know I'm staying and going with you all. I'm excited for them to know."

"Me too. Now, what about our trip? Where are we going?"

"Is your passport up-to-date?" she asked.

"Yes, ma'am, it is. If I'm going to need a passport, I hope it's to someplace with you in a string bikini for the whole week!" Clayton jested.

"I'm thinking about packing bikini's only with perhaps one or two dresses, but not many."

"A woman after my heart! I love you. Where are we going?"

"We are going to Sandals Montego Bay. It's an all-inclusive, couples only resort. You secured care for Brooklyn, right?" she asked.

"I can't wait to marry you. I'm just putting it out there. We haven't talked about it, but I cannot wait. I love that your immediate concern is for Brooklyn and Zoe. Yes, my parents are coming in from Florida the same day that we're returning from the beach. They have lots of plans for her for the week. Brooklyn can't wait for them to get here."

"Being your wife soon means as much to me as it does to you. We'll have the week away to talk about it. You know I love Brooklyn as much as I love Zoe. Knowing that they're going to be sisters one day will be the best news we could ever give them."

"I can't wait. You have what you need from me to finalize everything? I gave you my AMEX card to cover everything and you have how my name is listed on all of my identification. Anything else?"

"We're all set. I'll bring your card back when Zoe and I come over tomorrow night. I'm still salty that you wouldn't let me help with the cost," she said.

"You can get us next time. I wanted to take you away. I thank you for handling all of the planning. We're a team, baby!"

"Yes, we are."

"Oops, I need to jet. Michelle is calling. I better take her call. She's been on the phone with Brooklyn for the past hour. Maybe this is your chance to tell her about us?"

"Good idea. I'll do that. I'll call you late, late tonight. I can't be with you but I'd like to know you're naked and thinking about me when we talk. You game?"

"Always when it comes to you. Talk to you tonight."

**

Clayton inhaled deeply before he connected with the call from Michelle. He always had to prepare himself for any conversation with her.

He was about to say hello when her outside voice seared into his brain.

"Who is this woman who is the mother of Brooklyn's new friend, Zoe?"

Exhaling, he prepared himself to have the conversation he knew that sooner or later, he and Michelle would have to have. She's not a very active participant in Brooklyn's life, but she needed to know about him and Donna."

"I was planning on talking to you about that. Catching up with you has been a task lately. You've cancelled out on the last two visits with Brooklyn."

"Do not change the subject. We'll get to that in a minute because I told you I haven't been in Chicago lately. Let me tell you all the things Brooklyn told me not knowing what she was saying."

"Michelle, don't start."

"You already know. So, Zoe's mother? Her name is Donna? Is this the Donna I think it is? Tell me I'm crazy and you have not hooked back up with her."

"First of all, calm down and I'll explain. Brooklyn met Zoe at camp."

"She told me that already."

"Turns out that, yes, Donna, who I was engaged to back then is Zoe's mother. It's a coincidence that the girls met and became friends. I was surprised to see Donna."

"That's some coincidence. What does all of this mean? Are you seeing her now? She doesn't have a husband?"

"She's divorced like I am."

"Hmm. I guess she didn't love her husband like you didn't love me."

"Don't go there. Being petty is not a pretty look on you."

"You didn't answer my question. Are you seeing her?"

"Yes, I am. We've been seeing each other for a few weeks and no, Brooklyn does not know. She also doesn't know about my history with Donna. What did you say to her?"

Clayton quickly stood from the chair in his office feeling panicked. Had Michelle revealed their past, confusing Brooklyn?

"I didn't say anything. I was too busy listening to her tell me all the wonderful things about Zoe and her mother. It seems they have had more than a few playdates together. I assume you and Donna use that time to have your own playdates? How ironic is this? You're back with your one and only love."

"I don't want to argue with you, but my personal life is no concern of yours. I don't get in the middle of your personal life."

"Oh, yes you do. You get in the middle of my life all the time wondering who I'm seeing or who I'm living with. Every time I want to take Brooklyn someplace, you give me the third degree! I don't get to question you about your life?" Michelle yelled.

"I question you because when my daughter isn't with me and she's staying the night somewhere with you, I need to know who is going to be around her. We have one deal and that is unless you are serious about someone, you are never to take Brooklyn anywhere to spend the night and there's another person there; *ever*. She's our daughter, not one of your friends. I shouldn't have to issue you instructions for having men around our daughter. I agree to the same thing. I have been seeing Donna, but it's been on the sly. We've been testing the waters to see if we have old feelings that have become new feelings."

"And?"

"And the answer is yes. I'm in love with her and my plan is to make a life with me, Donna Brooklyn and Zoe. I'm going to ask Donna to marry me. I was planning to talk to you about this, just like I said. I would never have anyone around Zoe that I'm seriously interested in and not tell you. I would tell you, not out of obligation, but out of respect and consideration of you as Brooklyn's mother."

"Well, I have a new boyfriend that I need to tell you about. He's asked me to move with him to Paris. Since I'm not working right now, he helps with my bills."

"I offered you money during the divorce and you were too stubborn to take it. If you need some help, I can help you. I want to be very clear about something - you are not taking my daughter out of this country. We never discussed that and it's not happening. When she's sixteen, the two of you can make whatever plans you want. At eleven, you do not have my permission to take her to Paris. I hold her passport."

"Calm down, Clayton. I'm not asking to take her to Paris. I already knew you wouldn't go for that. Thanks for the offer about money. There were times that I wished I hadn't said no to what the court offered me. That's behind me now. I like this guy and I'm thinking about it. If I do, it won't be until next year and he was good with that. I didn't think you would let me take Brooklyn for a visit, so I'm going to stay here for now. Maybe you could bring her to visit me that way you wouldn't worry."

"I can definitely do that. She would love Paris. I'm sorry if I was curt. Images flashed in my head of her being in Paris and I'm in the states."

"I get that. You're protective of her and I understand. I also wanted you to know in case we visit the Texas and he comes with me. If you let me get Brooklyn at that time, I want you to know who's around her. I want you to meet him."

"I can do that anytime you like. I want you to be happy."

"Like you are now that you have Donna back?" she asked.

"Yes."

"Are you visiting soon? We're going on vacation for a week and the next week, my parents are coming to spend a week with her."

"No. He's a professional magazine photographer. He's in Brazil and I'm going to visit him in a few days. I'll be back within the month and I'll call you. I'll call Brooklyn to talk to her while I'm there."

"She'll like that especially if you send her pictures. She loves looking through books and magazines at foreign countries."

"Look, I'm sorry for hollering when you answered

the phone. The idea that you could be back with Donna was a shock, but I get it. You've always loved her. I'm happy that you're finally happy. I'm happy now, too."

"Michelle, that's all I've ever wanted for you."

"I'll let you go. Don't tell Donna hello for me. I'm sure she still hates me. Just know that I wish you and her well."

"We appreciate that."

"Dad! I'm hungry," Brooklyn said, suddenly appearing in his office doorway.

"Get you shoes. I'm coming. I better run. I promised her pizza and salad. Thanks for understanding. Have a safe trip to Brazil."

Clayton's body fell back into the chair. Conversations with Michelle can be exhausting. This was one for the books. It started out wild and crazy before leveler heads prevailed and they understood where they were each coming from. Hearing her wish him and Donna well was a surprise. He couldn't wait to tell Donna. She would get a kick out of that.

"Dad!"

Jumping up, he raced to get his own shoes on. He was suddenly starving and happy. The extra pep in his step told the story.

19

Donna watched as Zoe raced up the three front steps of Clayton's house, ramping up her excitement the moment Brooklyn opened the door. When they raced off, she smiled when Clayton filled the doorway. She leaned back on the hood of her car as he walked down the steps to join her.

"Hi there, beautiful. I would kiss you but little eyes might be watching," Clayton admitted.

"Hi and let me start off by saying, don't shoot me."

Donna contemplated what to tell him about tonight the entire drive over. They'd had such a lovely night of phone sex the night before and here she was about to ruin the mood.

"What?"

"I told you that I might have to make one last run to the hospital today. Looks like I do."

"That's okay, I understand. Don't sweat that."

"I know but I feel bad. We were going to talk to Brooklyn and Zoe tonight after we've had dinner. This was going to be our first time together and not just to pretend the only reason we're together is for those two best friends to hang out," Donna explained somberly.

"You're not going to be gone all evening, are you?"

"No."

"We can have dinner and a chat when you get back. I know how important Jack's case is to you. What did you tell Zoe when you packed your own luggage for the week? Wasn't she curious as to why you would be packing? We haven't told them you're going. They think Zoe's going on a trip with us," Clayton said.

Donna felt terrible. What she did was keep her luggage hidden from Zoe. They spent the entire day getting everything Zoe would need. Donna had packed her own bags the night before once Zoe was in bed. She then put her luggage in the trunk. She was hoping to still have the conversation before the end of the night. She had one issue at the hospital to take care of. She needed to do it before visiting hours were over.

"I know, but I have an idea. Zoe can hang out here with you and Brooklyn because she was going to do that anyway. She already knows she's going to the beach with you. My luggage is in the trunk of the car. Zoe's is in the backseat. You can take Zoe's luggage inside and tomorrow morning, we'll get mine out of the trunk. They will know by then that I'm going because when I get back, we're going to have a pow-wow of a talk with them."

"Are you sure you're not having reservations? You

can tell me if you are. I know this train has been moving really fast, but we aren't new to each other. I wasted a lot of time getting to this moment. I don't want to do that anymore. I know I want you."

"And I want you too. I love you, Clayton. I hope you're not doubting that."

"No doubts at all. Remember, I finally told Benny about us. I shared everything with him about my relationship with you. I literally cried on his shoulder for months when he and I met. I remember him once saying that he'd never heard anyone talk about a love so deep and compassionate the way I talked about my love for you."

"I'm glad he's okay with everything."

"He said that one day when there is a wedding, he expects an invitation. He also wants to meet you, of course."

"Of course. That's a given. We'll make sure he gets an invitation to our wedding."

Donna looked up at Clayton and saw the way his mouth curved up into a sexy smile.

"I'm happy to hear that. I know I've been the cause of us putting this chat with the girls off again and again. I didn't want you thinking it was because I had any doubts. I just wish I didn't have to go to the hospital the day before our trip. Like you said, I'm officially on vacation. I need to wrap this up. I was finally able to reach Carlotta last night. She told the truth to her husband and the child's biological father. The other doctors who are standing in for me are meeting me at the hospital so that we can go over the case as a group. She said both men would be there. I told her that she could be a donor, but she had already told her husband about her infidelity."

"Did she say how the husband took the news? I'm concerned about you getting in the middle of this kind of drama."

"I know, but I think it's going to be okay. When I talked to her this morning, she said her husband was calmer than she thought he would be. She said they talked and agreed that the only concern is the child."

"That's a strong man. I don't know if I could be that strong. She kept that truth hidden for a very long time."

"That she did."

"Her husband is okay with all of this with no fight?"

"I asked her again and again and she said his only concern at this point is the child. I shouldn't be too long. I'll call you when I'm on my way back and I'll even bring Chinese food for dinner. I already know the girls want shrimp fried rice. You can text me what you want. I don't think it will be too late, but getting them in pajamas and ready for bed would be good. That way we can eat and talk and once they're in bed all tucked in, we can snuggle up on the sofa. Do you realize that for the first time, we won't have to sneak around?"

"That means you're spending the night?"

"Nothing could tear me away from waking up in your arms in the morning. Besides, I have my luggage to put in your truck, I have an overnight bag for tonight. I'll grab that when I get back. I better get going. I told everyone I'd be there within the hour. I need to make one additional stop at the store. You have them covered until I get back or do you need me to help get them a little settled?"

"I'm sure they are in Brooklyn's room playing music, dancing or coloring or making some kind of jewelry or something. Let them have their fun. I'll get Zoe's bags and put them with Brooklyn's in my truck. Mine are there already. In fact, I can take yours now so that in the morning, all we need to do is get dressed and get on the road. I want to leave real early to arrive before everyone else. I want to be sure the house has been aired out and prepared for everyone's arrival. I gave the maintenance company a lot of instructions. They're meeting us there in case I find anything that they need to do before we all get settled in."

"I'm ready for tonight."

"The sooner you get going, the sooner you'll be back."

Donna watched Clayton walk around the car and open the back seat to grab Zoe's bags. She opened the trunk and waited as he lifted her luggage out. When she attempted to lower the trunk, her efforts were stopped as Clayton held it up where it was.

"I need one quick kiss to tie me over until you get back. They can't see us from the house."

Donna giggled and gladly obliged. As his head

came down to greet hers, she leaned up on the tips of her toes, anticipating the tingling feeling having his lips on hers would bring about.

He was making it hard for her to leave him. Knowing she wouldn't be long getting back to him is what would keep her going.

**

"Sebastian? What's up guy? If you're calling to blast me again about ditching you and the fellas the other night to play pool, I have already apologized a million times. I had a late night at the hospital and couldn't get away. Are you calling about tomorrow?"

"No, Clay, that's not it."

"Okay. I plan to get there early. I'll give you the other master suite. Selena and Reggie want the large suite on the first floor. I've got the girls tonight while Donna made a run to the hospital about an hour ago. Which are you calling about? To grill me or something else about tomorrow?"

Clayton was reclining in his favorite chair while Brooklyn and Zoe were laid out on the floor watching a movie in the family room. He told them they could watch one movie and then it was pajama time before they ate dinner in a little while. He was counting the seconds until Donna came back.

"No, no, that's not it."

"That's good to hear. What's up then?"

Clayton noted something not as jovial, but more sullen about Sebastian's voice. He was about to ask when Sebastian spoke up first.

"Listen, are you not watching the news right now?" Sebastian asked.

"Of course not. The girls are watching some movie about a girl who turns into her mother and a mother who turns into her daughter or something. I'm reading over a case study on treating burn patients. What's happening on the news? If I try to change the channel, the girls are going to scream and holler. You know how demanding Brooklyn can be," he laughed.

Clayton silenced himself a little more when the girls looked at him with scowls on their faces.

"Look, I need to tell you something, but don't freak out. You told me earlier that Donna was heading into the hospital and you just mentioned it again. I got a call from the head of security at the hospital. There's been an emergency that involves Donna. Don't panic if the girls are in front of you. Go to another room away from their little ears," Sebastian said.

Clayton jumped to his feet, knocking the folder he was reading to the floor and raced into the kitchen for privacy.

"What? What the hell has happened? Something happened to her?" he asked as the words rushed out, his breathing erratic. He was already in full panic mode, pacing around the kitchen like a madman.

"It's on the news but they are withholding the names. Listen, Donna was shot in the parking lot as she got out of her car. There is something about a man having an issue with his wife, the mother of a patient of hers? They were scheduled to meet with her. He was aiming for the mother, who was talking to Donna as they were heading inside of the hospital. It's some kind of domestic situation. Clay, the other woman didn't' make it."

Clayton couldn't breathe. His heart was beating so loud, the sound cascaded off of the walls of the kitchen.

"Donna?" he asked and held his breath.

"She was shot twice and rushed inside. You need to get to the hospital. It's bad, yes, but I need you to get there in one piece."

"The girls. I have the girls. What do I tell them? I can't take them with me when I don't know what's going on or how bad this really is," he explained.

"Brother, I can hear you breathing out of control. I need you to calm down. You can't do anything until you get there. I know you have the girls. That's why I'm pulling up to your house right now. I'm in the driveway. I'll look after the girls. Brooklyn is always saying she needs more time with her godfather and I'm here now. Get your keys, smile at them without upsetting them and come open the door. Tell them you have to go to the hospital. I promise to keep them away from any news, especially once word gets out of who the doctor is."

"How is she? Do you know? Any word on that?"

"No one is telling me anything. Mason, the hospital's head of security answered my text when I heard about it. I called him and asked. He knows Donna and mentioned one of the victims was her. He had no idea of the connection with her to you or to me. He was simply telling me the name. It hasn't been leaked yet, but you know how that is. Someone at the hospital will look to have their fifteen minutes of fame by blabbing to some media person. The door, Clayton; come open it."

Clayton hung up his phone and stood stoic for a few seconds, taking the time to gather himself. Donna had been shot. The woman he'd waited a lifetime for. The woman he loved more than life itself. The woman he never wanted to be without again. If the situation is dire, he wouldn't have a chance. He had to get to the hospital.

Fixing his composure, he walked back into the family room, grabbed the remote and hit the mute button to both girl's dismay.

"I know and I'm sorry. It's just for a second. Look, I have to run to the hospital, but I won't be long. Uncle Sebastian is here and he's going to sit with you until I get back," he explained.

"Yeah!" Brooklyn screamed.

When the doorbell rang, he watched Brooklyn jump up from her seat on the floor and run for the door.

"Don't you open that! You know better!" he yelled.

"I'm not. I just want to be the first person he sees when you open the door. I love my uncle Sebastian," Brooklyn yelled as she danced in placed with excitement.

Clayton shook his head while his mind was focused on how fast he could get to the hospital.

The minute he opened the door, he watched Brooklyn jumped into Sebastian's arms, their usual routine. In the next second, she was talking a mile a minute about her new best friend who was over for a sleepover and what they were eating and watching.

"Go, Clayton. I got this," Sebastian said, waving him off.

Clayton nodded, kissed Brooklyn on the cheek and raced through the house to the garage and hopped in his truck.

This couldn't be his life, he thought as he rushed, barely allowing the truck to start before he put it in drive and headed toward Children's Health Systems. He thought he was being granted a second chance to do the right thing. He prayed silently as he headed out of his Dallas suburban neighborhood and into traffic.

20

Driving like a madman, Clayton didn't know if he'd make it to the hospital in one piece. All he wanted to do was get to Donna. He'd never been so frightened or felt more alone in his life. He needed her to be alright.

His hands on the steering shook uncontrollably. Finding a comfortable position behind the steering wheel was hard. He wanted to be out and running to Donna's side. Disobeying the law, he sped through a few red lights, making sure there were no other cars around. Reaching an intersection with more than a little bit of traffic, he stopped and impatiently waited for the light to change. He needed help and he knew who to call.

"Call Patrick," he said and the car immediately dialed the only surgeon he wanted operating on Donna.

"Clay, I'm already on my way. I'm less than two minutes out from the hospital. I got you buddy; I got you."

Clayton tried to speak again and couldn't. For the

first time, he felt the tears roll down his face. It wasn't that he wasn't impacted by terror the second he heard that Donna had been shot, but since that moment, he'd been operating on pure adrenaline trying to get to his woman. He needed someone with him. He was holding in his feeling when what he wanted to do was scream. Hearing Patrick say he was already on his way helped Clayton pass some of his pain off to his friend.

"Aaaah!" Clayton screamed, releasing his rage so that he could concentrate.

"Brother, I got you," Patrick repeated. "I also called Marcelle and she's on her way too. You know she and I are each other's hands in any operating room. Hang up and get there. I need to call to get operating privileges, so I've got this covered. I've got Donna. Do you hear me? I've got her, Clay," Patrick said.

His friend was so calm, that it allowed him to calm and focus on driving. He hadn't said a word to Patrick, but he knew what to say in response to Clayton's silence.

At the next corner, Clayton was close enough to see the lights illuminating the name of the hospital. He didn't dare think of the speed in which he had to have been driving to get to the hospital in five minutes. As he got closer, there were sirens blaring, people running about and flashing lights lit up the night sky. He drove as close as he could to everyone rushing around. He saw where the police were flagging for him to backup, but instead, Clayton jumped out of his truck and he ran, flashing his hospital identification as he sprinted. It wasn't for this hospital, but that was still the code, especially in an emergency. It was all hands-on deck. Many standing around knew him, but the few officers who didn't see his ID or know him, rushed in his direction to stop him.

"Let him through! He's good – let him through!"

Clayton heard Patrick's voice and headed toward it. He was flanked by several other doctors and a few security guards.

"Clay!" Marcelle screamed and pulled him into her arms as they walk toward the hospital emergency entrance. Someone handed Patrick an iPad, no doubt with information on Donna's injuries and condition. Clayton did everything he could to keep from snatching it and reading it himself. It had to be about Donna.

"How is she?" he asked hastily.

"Where are your keys?" Patrick asked him.

Clayton felt his pants pockets and got nothing. He then remembered.

"They're still in the ignition."

"Pauly, get that truck parked in the garage and hold onto the keys until I find you later," Patrick said to one of the security guards who took off running without a second thought.

"Emergency room staff have her stable, for now, but she's going to need surgery right away. This is Dr. Tyler Shields. He's chief of surgery at the hospital. He was the first to get to Donna after it happened. He'll be assisting Marcelle and I with Donna's surgery. I've worked with him here before or trauma cases."

Clayton shook the man's hand.

"Dr. Myers," Dr. Shields said, acknowledging him.

Clayton knew him well.

"Thank you for looking after her," he said.

"Absolutely. Patrick called me while he was on his way here and told me the situation with you and Donna. She's one of our brightest stars here at the hospital. I recruited her myself. I've got my best team ready."

"Tyler, get that team to prep Donna. We can talk about the plan while we're scrubbing in. I need a minute with Clayton," Patrick alluded.

"On it."

After Tyler rushed off, Clayton crossed his arms and took in deep breaths to calm his nerves.

Patrick continued reading and Clayton couldn't be silent anymore.

"Well?" Clayton asked.

"These are the notes from the emergency room team. Brace yourself, my friend. Remember what I told you; I got this," Patrick said eyeing him.

Clayton nodded his understanding, but inside he was a total wreck. He wanted to see Donna, hold her, kiss her and tell her everything would be alright. The truth was, he didn't know if it would be, but he was optimistic. He trusted Patrick over everyone else.

"Donna was hit with two bullets."

Clayton inhaled and felt Marcelle grip his hand tight and held on to his arm."

"Okay. Did either hit any vital organs?" he asked.

"One entered the top part of her abdomen, shattering two ribs and piercing her spleen. There appears to be no damage to the stomach, the heart or other vital organs, but I'll know more once I get in there. That one appears to have gone through her and out of her back. There are other test results I'm waiting for from the body scan. I expect those any minute. The second bullet is lodged in her shoulder. I'm not as concerned about that damage as I am about the damage to her ribs and spleen. You know both are repairable. Once I have her in recovery, we'll keep her sedated for a few days with potent pain medication to ease the pain of deep breathing, especially when it comes to the damage to her ribs."

"This guy shot her twice?" he asked.

"Clay, from what I'm told, and these details are still sketchy, after shooting his son's mother, she leaped in front of Donna. Wait."

Patrick scrolled through the iPad.

"Okay, the woman's name is Carlotta Olmos. Her husband who shot her is Emilio Olmos. People nearby heard the woman scream the word no. She then took a lethal shot. Tyler thinks that the move by her may have saved Donna's life. From video footage that the police are still going over, jumping in front of Donna saved her from a shot to the heart. I don't know all the specifics about that. Tyler asked for information and that's what he was told given. He typed it in on the notes."

"The woman didn't make it?" Clayton asked.

"No, she didn't. She was shot three times. The shooter is in custody. Two doctors and an orderly, who were in the parking lot leaving for the night, tackled him to the ground once they saw what was happening. They picked Donna and the woman up and got them into the hospital while others held the man down until security and the police arrived. You saw the mayhem outside when you arrived."

"I know those names. There's a child involved," Clayton mentioned. He and Donna had talked about the situation within that family.

"A child? I don't see anything about a child?" Patrick asked.

Clayton saw him look as if he were about to jump into frenzy-mode.

"No, he's here, in the hospital on the transplant list. She was coming to the hospital for a meeting with the parents and the transplant team. Patrick, are the mother's organs viable? I know this may seem a little insensitive and I apologize for that. Donna told me about this case."

"Last I heard, she was just pronounced. You know each organ has a different sustainability after death."

"Her kidneys. The meeting Donna was going to have been about the mother being a match as a donor.

They were going to schedule the transplant. Can you check on that? If her kidneys are viable, can they be given to the son? Is that possible? This case has taken all of Donna's time for the past few months. The mother is a match."

"If it's the kidneys, then that's roughly thirty-six hours. I'm sending notes to the ER team right now to get her on support to keep her body functioning. I'm also emailing the trauma team to reach out to the transplant team. Do you have any other information?" Patrick asked.

"Nothing that I can think of. I need to call Donna's sister."

"I'll have someone check everything. I'm not on that case but I can see what I can find out and let you know. Marcelle and I need to scrub in. I'll get word out to you and her family as soon as I find out anything. Make your calls and most of all, pray. You know how we do. We believe in medicine, but we have a belief in a higher power."

"I'm praying right now for your healing hands. Go on," Clayton acknowledged.

"I'm all over this and I won't let you down. I don't make promises because as doctors, you know we should never do that, but you already know she will get my everything," Patrick explained.

Clayton nodded unable to speak knowing if he did, the weight of the situation would hit him like a ton of bricks and he wouldn't be able to control his emotions.

He had to hold on in order to get his thoughts straight.

"I need to make some calls. Her sister is in Fort Worth. She'll want to call her parents. Also, I need to call her ex-in-laws and her ex-husband. She's close with them. Zoe's father will want to talk to Zoe and pick her up from my house."

"Let me get you a nurse to help with all of that," Marcelle said. She waved a few nurses over."

"I need Donna's phone. Where are her things?" he asked.

"We have them," one of the nurses said. "I'll get her phone for you," she added.

Clayton looked through his phone for Candace's number. He remembered Donna using Candace's phone to call him a week back. Finding it, he paused, trying to calm himself knowing that he needed to remain in control as he talked to Candace. She needed to be the go-between for the rest of their family which included Benny and his parents. He looked up just as Marcelle and Patrick raced through the doubled doors that only doctors could go through. He hollered before the doors closed.

"Patrick, save my woman, man. You know what she means to me. This was my second chance with her. I can't lose her this way," Clayton whispered more to himself than to Patrick. His brain was exhausted with worry. He couldn't utter words over a whisper when everything in him wanted to break down and cry.

"I know I mentioned the observation room, but be

the family today. I know doctors are the worst at being on the other side of things, but be that family member today. Do not observe the surgery. Let me do what I do," Patrick said before he raced off.

Remembering what he needed to do, he pressed the send button and waited.

"Candace, it's Clayton," he stuttered out.

There was no doubt she heard something odd in his voice. He couldn't hide it.

"How bad is it?" she asked before he could explain. "I saw the news. When I didn't get a call or text from her, I immediately thought the worse. We have a code. Anytime anything happens that could impact either of us, hurricane, tornado and anything else bad, we call or text each other a special code immediately. That's our sign that we're okay. I heard there was a shooting at her hospital and I've been waiting for her code. When it didn't come and instead, I get a call from you, I knew. How bad?" she asked.

"I'm sorry, Candace. It's bad. She's being taken into surgery with two gunshots. Trust me when I say she has the best. He's the best trauma surgeon in the country."

"How worried should I be? I know I sound calm, but I have to in order to take in what's going on. My parents are going to want to know everything. I'm about to jump in my car now and head straight to their house."

"You should be worried. I won't lie. The unknowing is the worse. The doctors are still waiting on additional tests and scans."

"Where's Zoe?" she asked.

"At my house. Donna and Zoe were staying the night with me and Brooklyn tonight. We were going to tell the girls that we are in love and then this happened. When he looked up, he saw Reggie and Selena rushing through the hospital doors.

"Sebastian called us," Reggie explained as they got closer.

Clayton held up his hand to signal he was on the phone.

"I'm going to drop my daughter off with her father and then I'll pick up my parents. We'll be there in no time at all. I know you've got this. You'll do what needs to be done. You call me if there is any change in any direction. I'll call Benny. He'll want to get to Zoe. Does she know?"

"No. I wanted to leave that to you and your family. It wasn't my place. I'll text you my address. Drive safe. Tell security who you are when you get here. I'll give them your name."

"Thank you for being there."

The minute he ended the call, he felt Selena pull him into a hug.

"What the hell happened?" she asked.

"We got a call from Sebastian who said you needed us here at the hospital because Donna had been shot. My neighbor came to sit with the kids. We got right in the car. How is she? Any word?"

"Patrick was here when I pulled up. Sebastian had already called him. He's taking Donna into surgery."

"That's good. No one else has the skills of medicinal healing that he has. Marcelle with him?"

"Yes. I can't believe this happened. I need to know how this could happen here on hospital property."

No longer able to keep it together, Clayton dropped on his knees to the floor. Feeling Reggie and Selena's arms around him, he cried.

"I got you buddy," Reggie said.

Selena joined him on the floor and held on tight. When she began to pray, he closed his eyes and joined her. Donna had to be okay.

21

Candace weaved in and out of the cars, moving as if they didn't have a destiny in mind. She, on the other hand, had a purpose. Her sister needed her. They had both gone through ups and downs in life, but nothing this serious had ever happened. She was trying to hold her composure for her parents. She looked over and saw her mother, Sallie, tense up and gripping the door handle and the center arm rest like she was on a rollercoaster ride. When her father, Randolph, patted her headrest from the backseat, she eased up on the pedal. It wasn't until her eyes landed on the speedometer did she know she was heading toward one hundred miles an hour. There was no need to land them all in the hospital.

"Sorry about that," she said softly.

"No need to apologize. We're just as anxious to get to the hospital as you are," her father said. "I want to make it in one piece. I know you're upset, but slow down. Look at your mother. You're terrorizing her."

"I know. Sorry mom. You don't have to hold on so tight. I'm back down to the speed limit. I'm picturing Donna laying on some hospital gurney needing me."

"She's at the hospital where she works. I'm sure they're doing everything they can," Randolph said. Candace knew her father was being encouraging. He was always the strong one.

"Do you think I should call Clayton again to get an update?" she asked.

"If she's in surgery, I doubt if they'll have an update yet. We'll be there soon as long as you don't drive us oof the road first. He'll call if there is a change we should know about. When did Donna and Clayton reconnect? You sort of raced through that part after telling us what happened. Who would have thought that would ever happen?" Randolph asked.

"I was thinking the same thing."

Candace glanced again at her mother who was comfortable enough now with the current rate of speed to join the conversation.

"Mom, I know it sounds crazy, but I swear it's the truth. I think the reconnect was instant. You should hear her talk about him. It's like they realize what they lost before. They are more in love now than ever before. He's perfect for her. She's never been this happy."

"They've always been in love. Imagine trying to find love with someone else when the love of your life had been around all along. I'm happy for her and Clayton. I just wish she had told me," Sallie said, sadly.

Candace reached out with her free hand and gripped her mother's hand tight.

"Don't be upset. They needed some time figuring out what love looked like for them. They wanted to be sure before telling a lot of people."

"We're not a lot of people, Candace. I'm her mother."

"Mom, I know. She was planning to tell you and dad. You know how bad things had gone for her. She felt publicly humiliated. Her spirit was crushed. Most of all, on a whim, she ran off and married Benny. She wanted to take her time with Clayton this time around."

"You could have told me."

"I wanted to, mom. I really did. I needed to be the sister that Donna trusts with her secrets. This was a big one, but well worth it. She's so in love. Even though Terry and I had been thinking about getting back together, it was Donna's love for Clayton that made me see what rekindling love could be like. I'm dating my ex-husband because like Donna, I was always meant to be with him. I realized that once I got my head on straight."

"I know I'm being oversensitive. I am happy for her and you and Terry too. Really, I am. I'm just worried about Donna."

"I know, me too. We all are."

"I love her and whatever makes her happy makes me happy. I understand why she hasn't said anything. What happens if she doesn't pull through? She and

Clayton came all this way to find each other again and now this?" Sallie asked.

"We're not thinking like that," Randolph interjected.

Candace allowed a slow trickle of tears to fall from her eyes, not even caring to wipe them away. There would be more of them. She turned her attention to how strong she had been when she arrived at her parents' house to tell them what happened.

After getting the call from Clayton, she dropped Grace off with her father and headed straight to their house. She didn't want to have the conversation about Donna being shot, over the phone. She was glad she showed up in person. The minute her mother heard what happened, she collapsed in the living room. Candace was thankful that she was within arm's reach to catch her before she hit the floor. Once everyone relaxed, they got on the road to make the drive to Dallas.

"Zoe? What about her?" her mother asked.

"She was at Clayton's house. A friend of his is with the girls. I called Benny and he's already on his way over to Clayton's house to tell Zoe. He said he'd take her with him for as long as we needed. He asked about Donna's condition, but I didn't have anything else to share other than what Clayton told me. He should be at the house by now. She'll be fine. I told him to not take her to the hospital until Donna is out of surgery and in a room. Maybe even then, we should wait."

"We can help with her. My grandbaby needs me. I'm not leaving Dallas until I know Donna is okay. We need to get a hotel room," Sallie claimed.

"I know, mom. I spoke with Clayton again when I was driving to your house. He said you and dad should stay at his house. I'll come back and get you some clothes and other things you'll need."

"I've always liked him for Donna," Randolph said.

"Me, too," Sallie responded.

"Me, three," Candace added.

"The shooting? It was about a child, you said?" Sallie asked.

"Donna and I spoke about that. It was a tricky situation. She couldn't go into too much detail with me. She did say that she was concerned that the issues between the husband and wife could negatively impact their son's care. I was talking to her as she was driving up to the hospital. She pulled into her parking spot and told me she could see the child's mother walking toward her car. We ended the call so that she could get to her meeting and then get back to Clayton and the kids. I knew something was wrong when I saw the news and she didn't call me. She always calls when there is an emergency so that I know she's not in harm's way. It's either a call or a text. That didn't happen and then when Clayton called, I knew."

Candace could hear her own voice cracking. She was glad that they were a few minutes from the hospital. They would get answers soon.

**

Patrick raced through the hospital door and looked around for Clayton in the private waiting room. He raised his hands to calm Clayton since he was supposed to be in the middle of operating on Donna. There was no doubt his friend would think the worse.

"Clayton, I need to speak to you privately," he said. Moving to a space outside of the room, Patrick spoke pointedly because he was rushing.

"What's wrong? Is it bad?" Clayton asked.

"No, not yet, that is. Listen, did you know that Donna was pregnant?"

"What? Pregnant? How far along?"

"I'm figuring about six weeks. I called for the head of obstetrics to join me in the operating room. There were a lot of tests run on Donna before we cut into her. You know, we always run a pregnancy test on women who are still of child-bearing age. Donna's test came back positive. I had an ultrasound done and sure enough, there is a baby in there."

Clayton had to lean back against the wall to brace himself. Donna was pregnant.

"Will the baby survive the surgery?" he asked.

"You didn't know, did you?"

"I did not, but trust me, I'm not surprised. Whew. What's next?"

"I'm going to do everything I can to save the baby. It's tricky, but it's possible. Again, you have me and I'm working with one of the best teams of doctors around.

I couldn't have crafted a better set of doctors to be in that room. We're about to begin. Now that we know what we're working with, I'm going to take great care to save the baby. I want to keep you hopeful. I also need you to understand how risky it is at this stage of her pregnancy. The surgery isn't near the womb, but we'll have to change our plan of medicine and sedation for her. I'll keep you posted. I thought you would want to know before I began. Now, I'm going to go scrub again. Keep your cell on. I'll have a nurse text you updates. That work?"

"That's perfect."

"Congratulations, daddy!" Patrick hollered and rushed away.

Clayton knew that was the beacon of light he needed. There was no way the powers that be would take Donna and his child away from him. He thought back to the first night they made love.

"That's the night," he said to himself. "That was the night."

22

Clayton was exhausted, but determined to not leave Donna's side until she woke up. Three days after her surgery and she was still heavily sedated, as much as they could without harming the baby. His child was still thriving inside of Donna.

Knowing that she would be okay was the best news he could have received. Though Donna was now out of the woods, they were still closely monitoring the baby's health. At this point, he'd only told Candace about the baby as not to worry anyone else until they knew the baby was in the clear. Today's remarkable surgeons can perform miracles where years ago, saving a baby at six weeks with trauma to the mother was unthinkable. Patrick was the number one cardio god in the country. Where other doctors have failed when it comes to surgeries outside of their specialties, Patrick has always succeeded.

Checking out all of the machines beeping around him, he checked Donna's vitals once again, finding that she was still in the green; she was fighting, as he knew she would. He leaned down and kissed her on each cheek, taking great care to not touch the feeding tube in her nose. That sustenance was keeping her and their child alive. He smiled when he thought back to the first night they had gone out on a date and went back to her house. They had made incredible love to each other all night and well into the morning. He was sure their child had been conceived that night.

Holding her hand, he leaned close to her ear.

"Keep on fighting, baby. I'm here fighting with you. I'm not leaving this hospital even for a minute until you open your eyes and wink at me. Patrick said your ribs are healing nicely and he thinks they can reduce the medication that's keeping you under. He doesn't want to pump too much more into you with the baby. He's concerned the baby will become too lethargic to continue monitoring his or her growth. We have a boxer for sure. I'm already claiming it's a boy. I'll also take a girl boxer. As long as you and our baby are okay, I'm happy. That means you have to come back to me. We didn't get to this point of finding each other again and falling in love for you or our baby to slip away. Patrick said the surgery was tricky, but he's on the positive side that you'll be okay. People live without spleens every day. We're going to have a great life. We're going to get married, raise our girls and our new baby. Our life is going to be so good that we're going to think we're living in a dream state. I love you. I need you. Zoe needs you. Brooklyn needs you and this little one needs you most of all."

Clayton reached down and gently rubbed Donna's stomach through the hospital blanket in the area where he knew their baby was still fighting.

"I also want you to know that Jack, got a kidney transplant yesterday. You were right that his mother was a match. I'm sorry that she couldn't be here to know that he will survive because of her. They were able to keep her on life support long enough to remove her kidneys. Things are looking up. I'm keeping a close eye on his case because I know you would be if you could. The chances are great for his survival. The father is in jail and will most likely be there the rest of his life. His biological father decided he didn't want to be involved at all. Carlotta had no other family. Jack's social worker has been working around the clock to find any but it seems, she didn't have any family in this country. Trying to find any outside of it has been hard. He is in capable hands. You did good, baby. Focus on getting better and keeping our little one breathing."

He kissed her cheek again and sat in the chair next to her bed. Looking down, he noted the duffle bag of clothes Sebastian had brought for him from home. He'd been doing that since the first night. His friends knew that the only times he did were to eat, shower and change in one of the hospital shower rooms. He also stepped out when her family came to visit her. The hospital wanted no more than two people in the room at a time.

He was expecting her parents in an hour or so. With him vowing to stay at the hospital, they were able to go back to his house each day to rest and eat. With his own parents coming into town early, they were also staying at the house to look after Brooklyn.

Zoe and Brooklyn had been brought to the hospital for the first time the day before, but only for a few minutes. He smiled when he saw them holding hands as they stood at Donna's bedside. It was also the first day they'd seen each other since the shooting happened.

Benny had been by the hospital a few times and Clayton made sure to keep him up-to-date on her progress. Benny offered to help where he was needed. He was taking time off from work because what was most important was Donna getting better and him keeping an eye on how Zoe was doing.

His friends were delivering food to his house several times a day and transporting both sets of grandparents to the hospital when needed.

Hearing a knock on the hospital room door, he turned as Candace walked in.

"Hey. How is she?" Candace asked.

"Hanging in there."

"The baby?" she whispered.

"The baby is still good. They're giving her steroids to help with the baby's growth."

"Are there any long-term impacts to the baby?"

"Other than a possible issue with being smaller at birth and Donna possibly delivering prematurely, he says no. He's been consulting with the pediatric department head who is now on Donna's team. She's onboard with the course of treatment. I've been keeping up with everything. I'm in full support of the treatment plan."

"Thank goodness she has you," Donna said walking over to the bed.

"And you, too," Clayton said.

"I almost forgot why I stopped in. First, if you want to leave to shower and change, I'll sit with her. Thanks for letting me stay at your house too. It's crowded, but still roomy. Brooklyn showed me the extra bedroom on the other side of your man-cave. That's where I've been staying. I may not leave either."

Clayton chuckled as he stood.

"Stay as long as you like."

"One more thing, Michelle is here and asking to speak to you. She's in the waiting room. She was giving security hell trying to prove that they should let her up here to Donna's floor. I eventually had to go down and get her."

"What? Michelle who?"

Candace burst out laughing. It had to be from the outlandish look on his face.

"Yeah, that was my response too when a nurse called me to the phone to take the call from a crazy woman in the lobby demanding to speak to someone in charge. Whew – she's a pill to swallow."

"Tell me about it. Why is she here?" he asked.

"I have no idea. I'll sit with Donna. Perhaps go check before she reads the riot to everyone in this hospital."

He stood and walked out, walking right up to Michelle in the visiting room.

"Michelle?" he asked walking up to her.

"Clayton! Are you okay?" she asked.

He looked around and saw all eyes on him and walked them to a quieter part of the room.

"What are you doing here?" he asked.

"Brooklyn told me. I called to talk to her yesterday and she told me what happened. I was heading to Brazil, but when I talked to her and she started crying to the point that I couldn't understand a word she was saying, I knew something was wrong. Your mother came to the phone and told me the full story. Brooklyn needed me. I heard her crying like that and it scared the living daylights out of me. I got on a plane, flew in and went straight to your house. When she saw me, she leaped into my arms and held on. I sat down with her in my arms and she cried herself to sleep. I stayed with her. I'm here to help with her. I know your parents are here, but I'm here for her. I can't describe for you the fear that went through me when I heard her voice. Your mother told me that she had spurts of not being able to get Brooklyn to stop crying. I know I haven't done my best, but I needed to be here for her. How are you? How is Donna?" she asked.

"Thank you for doing that. I know she was happy to see you," he said.

"She was. I told her I was stepping out to check on you and she looked terrified. She told me that she was afraid someone would shoot me like they shot Zoe's mom. I assured her I was going to be okay and would be right back. Then this hospital wouldn't let me in. I'll let that go. I wanted to see if Donna was okay and if you needed anything."

"Looking after Brooklyn is enough. I know my parents love being here for her, but they could use a break, I'm sure. I appreciate you being here. How long are you here for?" he asked.

"For as long as you and Brooklyn need me to be. I thought I would take her mind off of all of this and spend a few days at the Hotel Crescent Court and do a spa day and some shopping. I thought I would check in for a few days and she and I could enjoy some fun. I also offered to take Zoe with us. Her father said it would be okay. I'm making sure you're okay with me doing that. I know I can be flaky, but like I said, I heard her crying and it tore me up. The way she leaped into my arms when I got to the house, I'm not going anywhere until I know she's okay. You good with that?" Michelle asked.

"I'm more than good with that. Thanks for the help. I was going to call Brooklyn after I took a shower and changed. She and Zoe will love going to the spa. If you need any money for the room, you can use my credit card."

Michelle held her hands up and didn't take the card he pulled out of his wallet.

"No worries and no need. My boyfriend gave me his card and told me to do whatever I needed to do with it. I've got this all covered. Are you sure you don't need anything?"

"Just prayers," he noted.

"I've got that. Donna's mother went with Zoe to Donna's house to get some clothes for the next few days at the spa. I'll keep them occupied so that they don't spend too much time worrying. There will be no television. Images of the hospital and blood on the ground is horrible. Brooklyn and Zoe don't need to see that. You focus on Donna."

They hugged and thanked her before she walked off just as Candace walked up.

"Don't worry – my dad is in with Donna. Mom went to the house with Zoe. Benny called saying Michelle is taking Zoe with her and Brooklyn to a spa for a few days?" she asked.

"Yeah. That's why Michelle came here. She wanted to be sure it was okay with me, and it is. I guess wonders never cease. She said she hopped on the first plane smoking to get here to Brooklyn."

"Well, aren't we all just one big ol' happy family!" Candace kidded.

"In a time of need, that's how it should be."

"Have you told anyone else about the baby yet?" she asked.

"No. I want to wait until Donna is woke. She hadn't told *me* about the baby. Telling others is something we need to do together."

"Go change. I told Sebastian I was going back to the house to get mom to bring her here when she and Zoe are done. I hear things are really looking up. Patrick came in right after you left. Is he on staff here?" she asked as they walked.

"No. He works with me. He was given full privileges here for Donna's case and Jack's as well. That's the little boy in the middle of all of this."

"How is he?"

"He's good after the transplant. Time will tell, though. Patrick said so far, there are no issues."

"What will happen to him after?"

"That's something I don't know. He will need a lot of care over the next year or so. I don't know if foster care will get him what he needs. It will take a special family since he doesn't have anyone else."

"No one?"

"The social worker couldn't find any family. The husband said she doesn't have any and since Jack, technically isn't his, he says his family isn't an option either. I don't know – it's crazy. It's a big mess, but right now, getting Jack that kidney was what mattered. I'm going to keep an eye on him and be there for him. Someone has to be."

Candace linked her arm with his as they walked.

"This is why my sister loves you. You are a great man, Clayton."

"Your sister is a great woman."

"When is the wedding?" Candace asked in jest.

"You may be joking, but trust me, the minute I can get us married, it's happening. I was going to propose on the beach. No matter. It will happen when she wakes up. Wait until you see the ring!" he declared.

"Yeah!" Candace chimed.

23

Donna's eyes opened slowly. She winced at the pain that seemed to be in every part of her body. How is that possible? Why was she in pain? Where was she? Her face felt funny as she tried to lift her arm to touch it and found that a movement that small was too painful and she stopped.

"Baby? Can you hear me? Donna? Look my way, baby."

Clayton? That was Clayton's voice. She could hear it, but couldn't see him. She tried hard to open her eyes, but they hurt.

"Remember, she'll be in a lot of pain. She shouldn't try to move too much too soon. She's been out for six days. I'm not sure she remembers what happened to her."

Patrick? Was that Patrick's voice?

"Donna? If you can hear me, don't try to move too much. I do need you to open your eyes again. Can you do that for me?" Patrick asked.

Why were her eyes so sore? Why did her nose hurt?

Her arms weren't moving without extreme pain. She tried to speak but could barely move her lips. Her tongue felt like a brick in her mouth. What was going on?

"Baby, it's me, Clayton. Can you hear me?"

This time instead of trying to speak, she used all of her might to get her head to move. She could feel a slight nod, but that was all she could muster up.

"That's good, Donna. We saw that," Patrick said.

"You're doing great, baby. You nodded. Take your time, but can you open your eyes again, even a little bit? Can you look at me?"

Donna pushed through the pain and opened her eyes slowly. As they focused, she could see Clayton's handsome face hovering over hers, blurry at first and then he came into focus. Was she laying down? As more of her surrounding came into focus, she knew where she was; she was in the hospital. She was in a bed. Was she a patient? Trying to focus on what Clayton and Patrick were saying, she tried to remember why she would be in a hospital in a bed.

"Baby, hold tight. It may be hard for you to speak. You've had a feeding tube in for almost a week. It was just taken out. You were also on a respirator, but not anymore. I know everything hurts. We're just glad to see you're awake. If you can hear me, squeeze my hand just a little bit."

Following Clayton's words, she tried to move both of her hands because she didn't know which one of her hands he was holding.

"Fantastic!" Clayton declared.

She was waking up even more and then it hit her. She remembered why she was in the hospital. There was a shooting. She had gotten shot. Images poured in. She ended a call with Candace and got out of her car. Carlotta walked over to her. It was evening and the parking lot was dark. There were others walking about talking and walking to and from cars. She and Carlotta had taken a few steps toward the hospital entrance when Carlotta's husband race up to them crying. He didn't speak a word. He started shooting. She remembered feeling a hot sting in her chest and then her shoulder. After that, she only remembered the darkness and the pain of hitting the concrete. She'd been shot. She and Carlotta had been shot.

"I know it hurts. Try to breathe, Donna. You were shot. Do you remember that? Two of your ribs were cracked. Breathing may be hard, so take it slow and easy while I check you out," Patrick said. "Nurse, can you call Dr. Denise Cole, the head of obstetrics? Tell her Donna Spencer is awake. I need her here immediately."

"Yes, doctor."

Donna heard it all. She suddenly remembered something else. She was pregnant. She had found out that morning that she was pregnant. She was planning on telling Clayton when they got to the beach. Telling him had all been planned out.

After everyone was asleep, she would ask him to

take her for a walk on the beach where she was going to hand him her positive pregnancy test. Her own doctor had confirmed what she already knew after taking three home pregnancy test three days before she went to see her own doctor. The baby! Her brain screamed the words, but nothing came out of her mouth. What happened to the baby? She started to cry. Though her body felt the pain of crying, her heart hurt even worse. Had she lost her and Clayton's baby?

"Donna? What's wrong? Are you in a lot of pain? Patrick, I think she's in pain," Clayton said.

She needed him to know that she could hear him and it wasn't the pain. It was the baby. She took her time and tried to form the words.

"The baby," she stuttered out. "The baby," she said again.

"Donna, the baby is fine. Patrick, Marcelle and your entire neonatal team have put everything into the care of the baby. Baby Myers is a trooper. Don't cry. The baby is fine, right Patrick?" Clayton asked.

"Yes, the baby is doing good. Still a little, tiny nugget, but holding on. This baby wants desperately to be a part of this family. I need you to relax and stay as still as possible. You'll find it hard to breathe, but I need you to work on that. You've been under as long as I could keep you. For the baby's sake, I need you woke and breathing on your own. Can you do that for me?"

Donna nodded her head and relaxed back on the pillow. She could feel Clayton's hand in hers. When she felt him pulling it away, she gripped it as tight as she could.

"I'm here. I'm not going anywhere," he said.

She needed to sleep. Knowing that Clayton was there and that the baby was okay was all she needed for now. She allowed slumber to take over.

**

"This is your answer to a guy's night out?" Sebastian asked Patrick and Reggie. The four of them, including Clayton, sat around one of the hospital cafeteria tables enjoying the full spread of food in front of them that Will delivered earlier. Everyone knew that Clayton wasn't keen on leaving the hospital for more than an hour. Patrick had come up with the idea to have some good food delivered. In the quiet of the hours after the cafeteria closed, they tried to provide Clayton with a chance to exhale now that Donna's condition was improving. Best of all, she was awake.

"Hey, don't look a gift horse in the mouth. Look at all of this food Will cooked for us. There's fried chicken, porterhouse steaks, steamed and fried shrimp and the most tender beef brisket I've ever had," Patrick stated, making his point clear when he took his fork and dug it into the center of the tray of meat.

"Let's not forget the Italian roasted potatoes, green beans with smoked turkey and buttered squash, all of Clayton's favorite dishes," Reggie added.

"You guys know I appreciate this just as much as I appreciate you. You've been here with me at some point in the day every day that Donna has been in the hospital. I can't thank you enough or Will for all of this food. It's a good thing the cafeteria is closed or we'd have people rushing over to us for a taste."

"He sent over a couple of crab cakes too but there's only enough for you. I'll put those in the freezer at the house for when you develop a real appetite," Reggie said. "How's Donna doing today? Selena was planning on coming by but she took the kids over to visit with Brooklyn. I hear club sandwiches are on their menu tonight."

"Everybody has been front and center this whole time. I haven't had to do or worry about anything at home thanks to all of you. Donna is doing better. Patrick woke her up earlier today."

Clayton looked to Patrick as he contemplated sharing more.

"That's right. It was time to see how she was feeling. We could only do that by asking her. She's in pain, but it's bearable, which was my concern."

"That wasn't the only reason," Clayton said. He knew it was time.

"Oh?" Sebastian asked.

Clayton looked Patrick's way again, for support.

"You have the floor, my brother," Patrick acknowledged.

When all eyes turned to him, Clayton leaned back in his chair and smiled like the proud dad-to-be that he was.

"Before Donna had surgery, Patrick shared the news the pre-surgery tests, they found that Donna is pregnant."

"Really?" Sebastian shouted. Clayton reached for him and caught his chair just as Sebastian almost tumbled backwards out of it to the floor in all of his excitement.

"Yes, really," Clayton happily acknowledged.

"How far along?" Reggie asked. "That's wonderful news."

"She's racing towards eight weeks this week. Our miracle worker here and his very talented wife saved not only Donna, but they saved the life of our child."

When the guys started pounding on the table as if they were hitting drum sets, for the first time in two weeks, Clayton felt like his old self. One staple for them was when they celebrated a success for any one of them, they pounded the table.

"This is amazing news, brother. Is Brooklyn stoked about being a big sister?" Sebastian asked.

"We haven't told anyone else other than her sister and all of you. I wanted to wait until Donna was awake so that she could tell her family. We are going to tell Brooklyn and Zoe at the same time. You each should know that I'm going to propose, something Sebastian already knew. I told him I was going to do it at the beach. Since we didn't go, I'm going to come up with another plan."

"Life back on track," Reggie said.

"Back on track," Clayton agreed. "Thanks for being my brothers through everything. You guys keep me standing tall. You correct me with my mess and you celebrate me; we celebrate each other. I couldn't ask for a better group of brothers that my parents didn't give birth to."

"I'm wondering who's going to be the godfather. I'm Brooklyn's godfather and you know I have an expectation with the new baby," Sebastian said, patting himself on the back the best way he could.

"Hey, we have to share Clayton's kids. Not that I think this baby will be the last one," Patrick added.

"What I was thinking is that all three of you could stand as the baby's godfathers. There is no such thing as having too many role models. What do you say?" Clayton asked, searching each of their faces.

"Yes!" the guys all said together.

Finding his appetite after revealing his secret, Clayton reached for a plate and began piling it up with food.

"Take your time and eat. Candace is going to sit with Donna until you're ready to go back. Relax and let us catch you up on what's been happening out in the world. I know you've avoided the news on the shooting, but we thought you'd like to hear the latest from us. Reggie was able to reach to the district attorney, who is a personal friend of his, to get an update. Are you ready to hear it?" Sebastian asked.

"I'm ready. You're right, I've been avoiding it. No

matter what the media are saying, the end result is still the same. Donna was shot and so was a very sick little boy's mother. Let's hear it," he said as he ate.

"It appears, the mother, Carlotta, never told her husband, Emilio, that the little boy wasn't his. She had to finally tell him because once he was tested as a possible kidney donor, he would find that the blood types for him and his wife could not have made their son. She finally told him and from what a friend of hers is saying, he was calm. He was upset, but not in a way that Carlotta thought he would strike out like he did. What made it worse was that the biological father, Hector, was one of the shooters best friends. He spoke briefly to some reporter about his connection to them and then he ghosted everybody. Emilio left a note explaining why he was doing what he had planned, which was to hurt Carlotta. His note didn't say how. From the way it was written, he had planned on doing something to himself, but that was foiled when some doctor's tackled him in the parking lot."

"This whole matter is sad," Clayton said. He spent days thinking about how bad things turned out.

"Right now, the husband isn't talking anymore. I hear he was quite chatty, but has since decided to invoke his right to remain silent," Reggie noted.

"Thanks for filling me in. I've kept the television off in Donna's room to make sure nothing about it comes over the air. There will be time down the road to talk to her about all of this. Am I selfish for hoping there won't be a trial because I don't want her to have to deal with any of this?" Clayton asked.

"Bro, not at all. You're looking out for her and that's admirable. I don't think that will be an issue. The DA mentioned Emilio is pleading guilty, so that means no trial. Let's hope that's the case."

"That's good. This whole scenario has been enough for everyone. Donna needs to heal and so does Jack. Let's eat and catch me up on happier news," Clayton said as he gazed to each man around the table.

"I've got some news!" Sebastian shouted.

"Okay, fine, I guess we're starting with you. What is it?" Clayton asked.

"I think I'm in love," he said.

"Again?"

Clayton laughed out loud when he, Reggie and Patrick said the same word at the same time.

"Look who is wide awake, finally!" Clayton expressed excitedly, entering Donna's hospital room. She was in her third week at the hospital and had been moved out of intensive care and into a regular room. He was happy to see her sitting up in bed, something her doctors told her that once she could, she would be closer to going home, something he was happy to know would be happening in another day. She would be leaving and recouping at his home. Being a doctor, he wanted to be able to look after her closely. Curled up in bed asleep next to her was Zoe, who was sound asleep.

"Me and only me. This one has been asleep for almost an hour. Benny brought her by as soon as visiting hours started. We agreed to let her stay the entire day with me, hence the huge backpack of books for her to read along with her iPad. She was on it for about five minutes before she fell asleep."

"She needed to be next to you to go to sleep."

"He said she hasn't been sleeping too well. We thought what she needed was a few hours of sleep right here with me. As you can see, it worked. I told you to go home and get more sleep than you've been getting sleeping in that chair."

"I love you," he said. "I know you thought that I would follow that instruction, but no. I wanted to come and bring you some good news, but first, how are you and our little baby doing?" he asked.

Though Zoe was asleep, they had already told everyone about the baby which was probably another reason why Zoe was clingier than usual. Once she was told about the baby, all she wanted to do was read to the baby every day.

"My doctor was here this morning and she said the baby was doing great. I thanked Dr. Denise for her help. My regular OB is on the case."

"How are you feeling? How is your breathing now that you're sitting up?" he asked.

"Much better. Guess what?" she asked.

"I'm listening," he said, taking her hand in hers and plowing it with feathered kisses all around.

"I was up on my feet again today. I actually walked up and down the hallway twice. Patrick said that was amazing progress. He wants my chest to stay wrapped because of the injury to my ribs, but they're going to loosen it up some so that it's not so tight. My breathing is good and I've passed all their test. I've also got my appetite back. They can't feed me enough. I can't wait to get out of here and get one of your grilled hotdogs!"

"You may be getting that sooner than you think. My

good news, that Patrick is allowing me to share, is that you will be able to go home tomorrow. He's going to examine you in a little while and run several tests. He believes you'll be fine to go home under my around-the-clock care."

"Around the clock? What about work?" she asked.

"Work? Woman – I'm not working anytime soon. I've taken a leave of absence. The hospital was already planning that before I went to the administration about it. There was no need to explain my plan. Your health, the baby, Brooklyn and Zoe are what's most important. Those girls have been planning for you to come home for days now. Wait until you see the welcome home decorations they are planning for you."

"Where's Brooklyn?" she asked.

"She's with Michelle. Can you believe she's still here? She meant it when she said she would stay as long as Brooklyn needed. She's been helping Brooklyn at the house with me coming back and forth. Last night, Brooklyn stayed with her at her hotel. They're going shopping for school supplies and she's getting Brooklyn's hair braided. She said she'd drop her off before visiting hours were over."

"We missed our summer on the beach."

"And our getaway that you planned for us. We'll have time to do all of that. The girls are going back to school soon. We'll plan around vacations and such."

"Remind me to thank Michelle for all she's been doing. Zoe told me about the spa day that turned into three days. She said Michelle took her to get her nails painted, with Benny's approval. I think she's fallen in love with Michelle."

"You know what, I think Brooklyn has fallen deeper in love with Michelle. She needed her mother for the first time and Michelle has been here for her. When they told her about the baby, she let them each buy the baby a gift, though we still have several months to go. They're excited."

"Benny and Michelle have stepped up to the plate. I don't know what to say," Donna said.

"They love their kids and they respect us. That's how it should be. We'll find a way to say thanks. I can't wait to get you home in our bed."

"Did you hear that I have to be on bedrest for the entire pregnancy?"

"Yes, and that's exactly what you're going to do."

"I had a whole plan for telling you about the baby. I know we had just gotten back together and it was sudden. I was frightened that it was too soon for us."

"What? Too soon? Never. All that, you know what, we were having, it was bound to happen," he said pointing to Zoe who was sleeping but still had curious ears.

"I want this baby so much. This baby will be a part of you and me. Him or her surviving is important and so I will do exactly what every doctor is telling me I have to do and yes, that includes you."

"You're good moving in with me and Brooklyn?

Have you talked to Benny about that yet?" he asked.

"He was here yesterday when you left early to take Brooklyn out for your daddy-daughter lunch. He said he was already expecting that considering he assumed we would be getting married. That was even before I told him about the baby. He's onboard with her moving into your house. He said if you need hands moving my and Zoe's things from my house, he would lend a hand."

"I'm letting Candace handle all of that. I wouldn't know what to bring and what not to bring. She secured two large storage units and is going to work with a realtor to rent your house. Your parents have already decided that they will take responsibility, along with my parents, to redecorate Brooklyn's room. The girls want to stay in the same room, though we have enough space for them to have their own rooms. They don't want that yet. They're too excited that they will be able to call each other sister soon."

Donna nodded, looking down at the gorgeous two-carat princess cut diamond engagement ring on her finger.

"Speaking of that, what are we going to do about the wedding with me being on bedrest until the baby is born?" she asked.

"Our mothers have that all under control. They are planning something at the house. Look, I don't want you worrying about anything. Candace will be over sometime in the next few weeks with pictures of everything from your house. You can tell her what to do with everything. In a few months, you and I will have a designer at the house to start working on what we want for the baby's room after we find out if it's a girl or a boy. None of that waiting until the baby's birth to find out. As soon as we can know, I want to know. I think it's a boy, but that's just me."

"Me too!" Donna yelled and then covered her mouth when Zoe moved but then quieted again.

"Did Brooklyn tell you the name of the baby if it's a boy? We agreed to let her and Zoe pick the name. They think it's a boy too. They would love a baby sister but they really want a baby brother."

"No. What's his name going to be?" Clayton inquired.

"Titan. What do you think?"

"I love it! Great, strong name. He's definitely a fighter – or she. What about a name if it's a girl?" he asked.

"MaKayla, with a capital K. They told me that the K being capitalized is important," she laughed.

"I love you, Donna. I swear we will get this right and be happier than either of us ever thought we could be."

"I have a question," she said.

"Okay, let's hear it."

"It's about Jack."

"Jack? He's doing fine after his transplant. He's been moved from ICU and the kidney is functioning great. He'll be here for another week or two before he's discharged. His social worker is working on a place for him to go."

"No family has yet to step up? What about his father?"

"I forgot his name, but he has signed over all parental rights. I understand that he had a lawyer prepare the papers. I hear he's back in Mexico. He's never known him and he said he and his girlfriend have four children he can barely afford as well as two other children he had before Carlotta got pregnant with Jack. He'll have to go into foster care."

Clayton knew the news would be hard on her. He watched Donna go through a myriad of emotions. It was hard to digest that at five years old, Jack had no one to care for him.

"What if he goes into a home and the family doesn't know how to care for him? What if he gets sick and they don't know what to do?" she asked.

"Baby, I'm sure they'll be careful about the family they select for him. I was told that the social worker is looking to work with families that have cared for sick children before."

"I'm sure she'll do her best."

The worry on Donna's face and in her voice was going to be with them for the foreseeable future. He didn't think she'd be able to rest without being certain Jack was being given the best of care. None of what happened was his fault and yet, he had no one. He had an idea.

"What if we take Jack home with us? I know it's a stretch. He would need as much care as you will need. I will be home with you already. Our best friends, Sebastian, Patrick and Marcelle are doctors. Selena runs a daycare and you know she accepts kids with special needs. We have her to lean on. He couldn't get better care if it was written in a book with a perfect storyline. The girls could get practice being big sisters. There would be a lot of paperwork, but with us being doctors, who would be better to care for him? I know it will be a rough set of months for you if you have to worry about the baby and Jack. If I can make that happen, does that seem like too much to take on? Just know that you have to stay in bed. Jack will come with his own set of doctors who will look in on him. Again, look who our friends are."

"You are too good to me. I've been thinking of that, but didn't want to put too much strain on you. You would have to get me and him back and forth for appointments. You'd have the girls. Are you sure it's not too much?"

"Don't you know that I would do any and everything for you?"

"I know. I don't want to put too much on you. You are about to go from a household of two to five. I want to take Jack home with us. No one can look after him like we can. I feel like I owe him. He doesn't have anyone. His mother is gone; the only father he's ever known will never get out of prison and his biological father doesn't want to step up. He's a baby, Clayton. He needs people around him who care; that's us."

"You're right that Jack needs a loving, caring environment and we can give him that. We'll get him over the hurdle while his social worker takes the time she needs to find him a family that would adopt him; not just a foster home. How's that?" he asked.

"That's perfect."

"Get some sleep before the doctors come in poking and working you over in order to release you. I'm going to see what I can do about what's needed to be Jack's foster parents. I'll be back in a little while when Patrick comes."

"I love you, Clayton. I don't know if there are enough words in the English dictionary to describe how much I love you."

"You know how I feel. I've been saying it from that night of our first date when I believe the baby was conceived; it should have been you. It should have always been you and now, it is. I love you, too."

Epilogue
One Year Later

The courtroom was buzzing with chatter with every seat filled along the long wooden benches. People were even lined up, standing along the walls. The side door within the room opened as everyone stood while Judge Carla Montoya entered and took her seat. Donna grasped Clayton's hand a little tighter knowing that the moment was finally here.

As the judge began speaking, she looked to Clayton where their five-month-old son, Titan, bounced in his arms. The moment he heard the judge speaking, Titan tried to babble louder than she was talking. Everyone laughed.

"Looks like you have a future judge on your hands. I see he's in control," she said. "Why don't you and your family come forward as we get to the main reason for today," she said. added.

Donna, Clayton, Brooklyn and Zoe stood, moving closer to where the judge sat, but someone hadn't moved.

"You, too, Jack," Donna said.

Donna moved and reached for Jack who was as much a part of her family as any of them.

"Yes, Jack, especially you. We are here about you today," Judge Montoya declared.

One thing they discovered about Jack is that he was extremely shy, except when it comes to being with Clayton. Donna took Titan from his arms as Clayton reached for Jack and lifted him high up on his shoulders. That got a big, bright smile out of the six-year-old.

"I must say, I have been a judge a lot of years and I've overseen many, many adoptions. This is the first time in my career that the entire courtroom was filled with supporters for one case. I can usually look out and see several families grouped together by case, but in this instance, all of you are here to support Jackiel Daniel Olmos, known as Jack, and the Myers family. We actually had to move the other families to another courtroom to wait until we're done. I am excited beyond measure with the showing of support. There are a few people that I'd like to ask to come and stand with the family, per their request. The court recognizes all of you and we thank you for signing the pledge drafted by the family declaring your love and forever support as Jack's village. Can I have Dr. Sebastian Larsen, Reginald and Selena Jordan, Drs. Patrick and Marcelle Castle, Randolph and Sallie Johnson, Candace and Terry Parker along with little miss Grace and finally, Marie and Thomas Myers. Clayton and Donna wanted you close to them for the ceremony today. I'm calling today's adoption a ceremony because I like for them to seem less formal. Before I begin, I understand there are two young ladies who would like to read something they wrote?"

Clayton watched Donna help move Brooklyn and a very nervous Zoe to the front.

"Go ahead and read your paper from you and Zoe," Donna encouraged.

"Good morning. My name is Brooklyn Myers and this is my sister Zoe Spencer. We want to say that we love our brothers, baby Titan and Jack very much. Jack is very special to us. We like reading to him and playing with him even when he messes up our room with his toys. Me and Zoe want Jack to know that we will always love him. He was our brother the day our parents brought him home to live with us. Jack likes to ride his bike and me and Zoe like teaching him how to swim and roller skate. Today, everybody now knows that Jack is officially our brother. We are happy that he is a part of our family. Thank you," Brooklyn said.

She turned to Zoe and poked her.

"We love you, Jack. Welcome to our family for good!" Zoe added.

The claps and hoots from the crowded courtroom had to have been heard in other rooms in the courthouse.

"Great job. Jack is blessed to have such wonderful

sisters who love him."

"This is the moment I love the most. I hold in my hand the final adoption papers making sure that Jack will have his forever home. Dr. and Dr. Myers, the two of you not only took over his care, but you took him into your home making sure he knew he was loved and wanted. You didn't hesitate to reach out to the court to let us know that you wanted to make Jack a permanent member of your family. Watching you from the bench, I can see how happy Jack is sitting on his dad's shoulders. He's healthy, happy and loved. The court can't ask for more than that. If the two of you will step forward, I need your final signature on these documents. One is final adoption papers and the other is to officially changed Jack's name from Jackiel Daniel Olmos to Jackiel Daniel Olmos-Myers. By your wishes, he will keep Olmos in memory of his mother.

Donna handed Titan to Sebastian and joined Clayton at the desk. Once they both signed, everyone again cheered as Clayton pumped his fist in the air and watched Jack do the same thing. They were officially a family of six.

"Good luck to you all. Thank you for helping the number of children waiting to be adopted get decreased by one."

"Thank you," Clayton and Donna acknowledged.

As everyone gathered around them, family from near and far and more friends than they remembered they had, Clayton put Jack down where he quickly grabbed Brooklyn's hand. He asked Sebastian to get everyone gathered outside for pictures.

Left alone, Clayton pulled Donna close.

"You know, we've had a lot of highlights in this past year. From your healing, to Jack's successful surgery to Titan's birth to taking care of all of our kids and the home. It all led to this day. I never could have survived all of this without you. It had to be you. I want to thank you for being my best friend, my love and most importantly, my wife. I thought getting married in our home six months ago was the top of the heap. Our love continues to amaze me. Are you ready to go home and enjoy our family of six?"

"Six? That number is unthinkable considering I went from being a mother of one to a mother of four in one year. I wouldn't change a single thing about it."

"I wouldn't either. I love you, Mrs. Myers and I look forward to a lifetime of love and family."

"And more babies?" Donna asked.

Clayton chuckled.

"You want more babies?"

"I do. I didn't know I wanted more until I realized we have four and I love them with everything in me. I would love to adopt another child. There are so many children in need of homes. I wish we could adopt them all, but I know that's not possible. Look at how we love Jack. Most of all look at how much Brooklyn and Zoe love him. They never missed a beat from the first day. I'm not saying I want to do it today, but it's something

I want to leave the door open to."

"You don't need to convince me. We are in this together. Did you see our village today? This is what life is about. I couldn't have had this with anyone else but you. What have I been telling you from the start?" he asked.

"It should have been me."

"Right. It should have always been you and now, it is. Let's go get some photos with our kids and the village and then we are taking two weeks of peace and quiet with the kids at the beach house."

"Yes! I can't wait!"

Hand in hand, they stepped out into their forever. It was a long time coming – but eventually, it did because it should have.

****New Series Alert****
Preorder today!
An Unexpected Destiny

Destiny Lockhart's high school crush, Lincoln Cole, is again front and center in her life. She last saw him fifteen years ago when she threw him out of her bedroom after their one night together following the senior prom. What should have been a memorable night had turned out to be her most embarrassing moment, leaving her feeling ashamed and undesirable.

There was no way entertainment mogul Lincoln Cole could ever forget the shy, yet beautiful butterfly that was Destiny from his years as a high school football star. The now feisty, sexy and self-confident executive who dripped in vibrant, dazzling appeal reminded him that they were never meant to only have a one-night-stand. They were always destined for forever.

For years, they lived on two different coasts unaware that soon, their past would become an unexpected present filled with unfinished desires that once looked like rejection.

Check out the first book in a new romantic series, "Sister Act", with book one, *An Unexpected Destiny*! Preorder your copy today at

Preorder Alert
It's Christmas in July!

The Christmas Layover

Preorder this July 4, 2022 holiday romance on Valentine's Day and enjoy a Christmas romance in July.

Get the early bird price of $.99 for preorders only. Price will raise to $4.99 on July 4th.

Millionaire Edrick Stone's plan to spend the Christmas holiday alone at his villa in Spain was derailed by a sudden snow storm that hit Denver, Colorado just as he was leaving. He couldn't be mad at the storm when he discovered friendly passenger across the aisle was also stranded, much to his delight.

Danica hated Christmas; even her friends secretly called her Scrooge. She carried a secret pain that resurfaced each year with the holiday until a mysterious stranger on a plane offered her the chance to have a very merry Christmas. She decided to throw caution to the wind and live in the moment.

Edrick and Danica had their own reasons for avoiding Christmas, but this year, they would find that the holiday wasn't meant to be spent alone, but in arms filled with love and possibilities.

****Upcoming Preorder Alert****
On the Right Track, Book 3 of
The Sullivans of Montana

**Preorder on February 14, 2022,
Valentine's Day**

On the Right Track

Dayton Sullivan is the youngest of the Sullivan boys and has found himself in a bit of a jam when he falls in love with Kima McDonald, the daughter of a man who could be responsible for the death of Kima's mother, the woman whose fortune Kima now holds in her hands that her father wants to gain control of.

Dayton and Kima run off to the Sullivan Ranch in Montana in order to escape the life she's being told she has to live according to her father's schemes.

Can their love sustain them through the ups and downs they'll face against her sinister father or will and those he is indebted to find a way to get Dayton back on the race track and Kima married to a man she doesn't love, but who holds all the cards when it comes to her future?

Dive into book 2 of The Sullivans of Montana, "The Way You Love Me"

Now Available!
The Way You Love Me

Montana ranch owner, Perry Sullivan, befriended a woman who finds herself in dire need of his help. He doesn't hesitate to provide shelter and protection the way any man should for a woman who is in distress. What he had not planned on was in the midst of the turmoil that was her life, he would lose his heart and fall in love while at the same time putting the lives of his own family at risk.

Gizelle Duncan had a tumultuous past she didn't want anyone to know about, but when that past, in the form of her abusive ex-husband, shows up in her life again, she has no choice but to accept help from one of those sexy Sullivan boys from the Sullivan Ranch. She thought she had lost all faith in real love until Perry showed her that she could trust him not only with her life, but with her heart.

"The Way You Love Me" will take you on a journey from the ashes of Gizelle's burned-out house and life and into the flames of passion that will not be contained even at the peril of a jealous ex-husband out for revenge.

Unforgettable

Baltimorean Reagan Kelly was expecting an uneventful weekend in New York City visiting her sister between Thanksgiving and Christmas. Though in the holiday spirit, the last thing she thought she'd find on a cold, wintery night was a chance at romance. Two days in New York City for business and a chance to see his best friend was all Crime Novelist, Keith Jackson had time for, or so he thought. He soon found time to extend his stay when the chance of a lifetime to spend four incredible days with the most beautiful woman he'd ever encountered landed at his feet. An unforgettable weekend is one thing, but can that weekend turn into a lifetime of unconditional love for Reagan and Keith, two self-professed workaholics, who didn't have a reason to slow down and smell the roses until now?

Seize the Moment

Aubree Campbell played a childish game with love and she lost. Ending her relationship with her live-in boyfriend, Russell Hall, because they became passing strangers in the night didn't have him begging and pleading for her to give him a second chance as she had hoped. Instead, the indomitable Russell made plans to move out and give her the space she desired, and then a world pandemic hit and they agreed to ride it out together under one roof.

Tensions brewed and so did their undeniable desire and passion for one other. Will their steamy nights lead them back to being on the same page in life and in love or will past hurt and jealousy return to put an end to their rekindling?

The Power of Seduction

Bakery owner Raquel Hastings assumed her relationship was perfect in every way, both in and out of the bedroom where she had enjoyed the most tempting, titillating, and out-of-this-world sensual romps between the sheets with sexy engineer, Preston Sharpe, a man who knows his way around a woman's body. That was until he took a job in another country which left her only with memories and intoxicating desires to be loved like that again. Her world had been turned upside down until the day he returned with a plan to turn her world right side up.

Preston's alluring visions of Raquel haunted him at night, alone in his bed in a foreign country without the woman he loved. With the chance to return home and to her loving arms, he dreamed of once again sharing nights of satiating passion that only two hearts meant for each other could share. He knew he had to ready his game of seduction if he were ever going to again have Raquel back in his life and in his bed. This time, his plan was to make it last forever with the hope that Raquel could forgive him and give their love another chance.

Make sure you check out book 1, of "The Brothers of Chi-Town", *I Can't Let Go* – now available for download and in paperback.

I Can't Let Go

Carter Garrison vowed to love, honor and cherish his wife, Sienna, forsaking all others, something he forgot to do during a weekend of fun, bad company and poor judgement.

Sienna Garrison never dreamed her college sweetheart, Carter, whom she pledged her life to, would break her heart and when he did, she moved out and moved on - or tried to.

What better occasion is there than a friend's wedding to stir up old feelings and memories of love, intense passion and nights of sensual titillation. Gazes from across a room after almost two years apart revealed depths of love that had never died.

Seeing Sienna again reminded Carter of what he'd lost and he vowed to never let go by doing whatever he could to get his wife back even if it included begging and pleading. Is Sienna ready to forgive and take a chance on life again with the only man she'd ever really loved?

When Carter brings on the charm and turns up the heat, no woman is immune, especially Sienna.

Don't forget to snag your copy of book 2,
Swagger and Baggage, in "The Brothers of Chi-Town"
series – now available
Swagger and Baggage

It's not a coincidence that casino owner, Torrence Allen, ran into his college sweetheart, Reese Michaels again; it's fate. As his memories unfold, he had tried everything to keep her in his life and his bed back then and failed at both. She wasn't ready for him then, but he hopes she is ready for him now.

Reese Michaels never thought she'd see Torrence again. Their split in college was dramatic and hurtful and still, no man had been able to win her heart. She considered herself the permanent third wheel to friends who had found love and marriage.

Torrence's swagger has always won women over, but it's his baggage that's causing his life to spiral out of control. He messed up and found himself without the woman he has always loved.

About the Author

Cheryl Barton lives in Maryland and in her spare time she loves to read espionage, crime and romance novels, cook, watch Sci-fi movies, spend time with family and friends and enjoy Maryland steamed crabs. Cheryl is celebrating over 30 years as a government employee and loves writing romance novels when she's not working.

Cheryl is the author of over thirty-one romance novels, four inspirational novels and is proud of six book compilation projects with several other incredible women.

Cheryl was a 2019 Finalist for the Emma Award given by Romance Slam Jam and a 2018 Finalist for the Literary Trailblazer of the Year award by the Indie Author Legacy Award. Cheryl is a member of the Contemporary Romance Writers where she currently serves on the board as the secretary.

Connect with Cheryl Barton

www.cherylbarton.net
www.crbarton.com
www.amazon.com/author/cherylbarton

Instagram: @cherylbartonbooks
Twitter: @cbartonbooks
Facebook: @cherylbartonbooks